A ROUND IN SPAIN

a round in spain

Tony Elliott

The Book Guild Ltd.
Sussex, England

The Book Guild Ltd.
25 High Street,
Lewes, Sussex

First published 1993
© Tony Elliott 1993

Set in Baskerville

Typesetting by Raven Typesetters
Ellesmere Port, South Wirral

Printed in Great Britain by
Antony Rowe Ltd.
Chippenham, Wiltshire.

A catalogue record for this book is
available from the British Library

ISBN 0 86332 847 4

1

What an attractive looking man, Liz mused as she walked out on to the balcony in the hot Spanish sunshine.

She had walked down the steps from her apartment to the clubhouse at La Manga at about twelve thirty, walked up to the bar and proudly asked for '*Agua con gas, por favor*'. Her Spanish was extremely limited but this was a phrase she had mastered and the water without gas tasted very flat. Pedro passed over the half litre bottle with a tall glass half filled with ice and flashed his white teeth.

'Thank you madam, one hundred twenty pesetas please,' he said in almost perfect English. He could never understand why the English tried to speak Spanish when everyone had to speak some English as a condition of their employment to work on the La Manga complex, a sports and residential development on the south-eastern corner of Spain about sixty miles south of Alicante. It had been the dream of an American called Greg Peters and he commenced development in the early 1970s. It extended to about 1,200 acres and incorporated two and a half golf courses, tennis courts, air conditioned squash courts, bowling rink, endless swimming pools, riding stables, a beach club about four miles away on the Mar Menor, a large stretch of almost inland sea, with facilities for sailing, wind surfing and water skiing and there was even a cricket ground which doubled up as a practice ground for the golfers. Liz and her husband, Tom, had bought a small apartment in one of the original buildings, a stone-faced block of flats set high on a hillside overlooking the South course about three years before and came down for a couple of weeks holiday once or twice a year.

Liz paid for the water carefully leaving a five peseta tip and took a seat at a table close to the attractive looking man. She had a good view looking over the course with its two thousand palm trees, verdant fairways, lakes and beyond them a large lemon grove with the Mar Menor in the distance with its backdrop of rather hideous blocks of flats and hotels on the strip, some of which were reflected in the mirror-like surface of the Mar Menor.

It was one of those perfect Spanish days without a cloud to be seen and hardly a breath of wind. Tom was out playing golf, having started at about eight-thirty and he should be in soon dying for a beer and full of *bonhomie* if he had won but not so happy if he had lost, full of complaints about the amazing good luck of his opponents.

Liz looked down the eighteenth hole to see if she could see him but the golfers on the hole were of very indifferent standard making her feel that perhaps she could do as well, especially when one of the four, an elderly woman of very ample proportions, hit her ball about five yards into a bush right in front of her.

'It really makes one feel one should have a go oneself,' Liz said half to herself but conscious of the fact that the man on the next table would hear.

'Why don't you?' he said immediately.

Liz looked at him more closely. About my age she thought, fair curly hair with just a touch of grey near the temples and above the ears, blue eyes, well tanned and not an ounce of fat.

'Oh, I'm no games player – I'd probably miss the ball altogether – besides I haven't got any clubs.'

'That doesn't matter,' he said. 'I happen to be a golf pro and I can certainly lend you a few clubs. I tell you what, come down to the practice ground tomorrow at ten and I'll give you a lesson, no charge and no obligation but if you like it we can take it from there.'

'That would be wonderful,' Liz heard herself saying. 'I'd really like that.' But inside she was thinking this is crazy. Tom was a good player, he could give her a lesson anytime but here she was arranging a lesson with a complete stranger: what was Tom going to think? Things had not been too good between them for a while and this holiday was supposed to bring them closer. Was this going to help? She would mention it to Tom and see what he said. She could always cancel it she thought.

Just then she heard Tom's deep booming voice. '*Caballero, cuatro* beers *aqui* chop chop,' in his typical mixture of English and Spanish which Liz found so embarrassing. He always forgot to say 'please' or *por favor* and the Spaniards were such a polite race. Also the waiters hated being addressed as *caballero*.

Tom came out on to the balcony very red from the unaccustomed strong sun and his stomach hung over the top of his shorts.

'Hello, luv,' he said pecking her on the cheek. 'You OK for a drink? Golf went well – three thousand potaters to the good – must be better than working – the others will be out in a minute – Dick's a bit pissed off – three putted the last or they'd have saved the back nine – thought you were coming to watch the last few holes.'

'I thought I'd watch you play the eighteenth from here but I didn't see you.'

'Christ, Liz, that's the eighteenth on the bloody South course. I told you we were playing the North.'

Just then the other three came on to the balcony swiftly followed by the waiter with the beers.

The golf pro rose from his chair, smiled at Liz, mouthed 'See you tomorrow' and in a few strides vanished into the relative darkness of the bar.

Liz felt relieved. She would not have wanted him to mention the golf lesson before she had had a chance to talk to Tom. Besides she did not even know his name.

Then she heard Dick say, 'Wasn't that Tony Seddon? The pro from Sheringham?'

Harold replied, 'Yes, that's the chap. A real ladies' man. Specialises in women who don't play golf who get bored to sobs out here with their husbands playing golf for a sure four or five hours a day. He probably recognised me 'cos I had a bit of an up and downer with him a couple of years ago after he came it a bit strong with Margaret.'

Liz felt herself shiver despite the intense heat. At the same time she knew her neck and cheeks had coloured. This always happened when she was embarrassed. Even as a child at school she could never get away with anything as she always looked the picture of guilt whenever there was a question of someone having committed the slightest misdemeanour.

She heard Tom say, 'Better watch yourself, old girl. Didn't try anything with you did he?'

'Certainly not,' Liz replied. 'Mind you I'd only been here a couple of minutes before you arrived.' Why had she said that? Why hadn't she said he had suggested giving her a lesson tomorrow? What was she going to say to Tom now? Again she felt herself flush but hoped no one would notice or put it down to the heat and the fact that she was of menopausal age.

Tom said unkindly, 'Not surprised – expect he goes for the twenty- and thirty-year olds rather than middle-aged matrons.'

8

Gilbert leapt to her defence. 'I don't think that's fair, Tom. I think Liz is a jolly attractive woman and conversation is so much more interesting with one's contemporaries than those a generation younger.'

'I don't think it's the conversation he's after,' said Harold. 'Margaret is about your age, Liz, and he made it pretty clear to her what he had in mind so don't fall for his smooth talking or he'll have another notch on his driver.' The men all laughed uproariously. Another round of drinks was ordered and Liz just felt she had to get away. Here were four reasonably intelligent men and everything they had said so far had some sort of sexual innuendo. Before long they would get on to golf – that was for sure – first reliving the highlights of the game they had just played with much more emphasis on the bad shots that had been played rather than the good ones. Then inevitably there would be an argument about who was the best player in the world. Was it Ballesteros or Norman or Faldo and how did they compare with Hogan or Jones or Nicklaus? She had heard it all a thousand times before. She wished the other wives had been there but Margaret was having a massage, Sue was sunbathing somewhere and Jane played as much tennis as the men played golf. I don't know why I came down, thought Liz. She got up.

'Sorry but I've got a bit of a headache. I think I'll go and put my head down for an hour. Will you be coming up for some lunch, Tom?'

'No, I'll grab a sandwich here thanks. Dick wants a chance to get his money back so we're going to play again a bit later on. I'll see you about sixish I expect.'

'OK,' said Liz. 'Are we meeting up anywhere before going down to the Strip for dinner?'

'Oh yes,' said Harold. 'It's our turn to do the drinks this evening. Come to our place about seven thirty and we'll go from there.'

9

'Great,' Liz said. 'See you then. Enjoy your game.'

She walked through the bar towards the shop where yesterday's English papers normally arrived at about lunch time. 'I'll just see if I can get a *Telegraph*,' she thought. 'The crossword could be the highlight of my day.' She turned into the shop and there was Tony Seddon.

'I'm so glad to have seen you again,' he said. 'We never even introduced ourselves. My name's Tony Seddon and I'm the pro at Sheringham in Norfolk. I come out here for about four weeks a year, partly as a holiday but also to teach a few of the Sheringham members who think they would like a lesson in different surroundings and I have a few contacts from Germany and Sweden who I teach here also.'

Liz held out her hand. 'My name is Liz Waldren. I'm on holiday with my husband, Tom, and we're here for another week. We've got an apartment at Miradores overlooking the South course.'

She shook his hand which was cool and dry. His handshake was firm but not overpowering.

'I'm sorry I did not stay to introduce myself before but one of those men – Harold someone I think – and I had a misunderstanding a year or so ago and I thought it was better to leave.'

Liz looked up at him with innocent wide blue eyes.

'What kind of misunderstanding?' she said ingenuously, interested to know what he was going to say having just heard Harold's version.

'Oh God, this is difficult because you know the people involved but basically I think Harold's wife wanted to make him jealous and told him that I had propositioned her.'

'And had you?' Again those wide blue eyes held his.

'Certainly not. All I said was that I thought it must be

10

more fun being a masseur than a golf pro and I think it was taken personally. I didn't know that she has a massage practically every day. Anyway, enough of that – what are you doing this afternoon?'

'Well, I came here to buy a *Telegraph* and will probably do the crossword, maybe have a nap, probably wash my hair and be ready and waiting for my lord and master when he comes back at about six – or more likely seven.'

'Gosh, that sounds really boring. You could do all that at home. You're on holiday. Have you ever been down to the cove and gone out in the outboard, been dropped off at a deserted beach and been picked up two or three hours later?'

'No, I haven't but I've always wanted to. The trouble is Tom plays golf every morning and if he doesn't play in the afternoon he just wants to sleep off the beer he's had at lunchtime.'

She felt she was being very disloyal. Tom was not as bad as that, it was just that on holiday he seemed to do what he wanted all the time and they never had a day indulging her.

'How about it then?' Tony said. 'Go back and get your swimmers and I'll pick you up at the bottom of the hill in twenty minutes.' Without waiting for an answer he left the shop.

Liz bought her *Telegraph* for 220 pesetas: over a pound for a daily paper and it wasn't even today's, what extravagance, and walked swiftly up to the flat. She took off her clothes quickly, put on her brightly coloured costume, sundress over the top, sandals, sun hat, dark glasses, dabbed on some perfume, grabbed a towel, thought about her book, decided against it and picked up her handbag. 'I must pay my share of the boat' she thought, and walked down the hill to the main estate road. She looked at her watch. Eighteen minutes from when she left the shop. Tom would never believe it.

11

A sleek silver grey Porsche 944 pulled up alongside her, its exhaust making the deep throaty burble which was the distinctive sound of the world's best sports car. Tony leant over and opened the door.

'Glad you decided to come,' he said. 'I didn't wait for an answer in case you said no.'

They swooped past Los Altos, Los Molinos, up the hill and round the steep hairpin bends leading down to the cove. Tony drove fast but in no sense dangerously. He was in complete control of a car she knew was capable of 140 miles per hour on the open road. They got out of the car, Tony grabbing a cold box from the back and walked down the steps. A swarthy Spaniard was sitting on the side of the inflatable, smoking, but when he saw Tony a wide smile broke across his face.

'*Hombre, como estas?*' he said.

Tony replied fluently, '*Bien, muy bien, y tu Paco, que tal?*'

They embraced and after a few more exchanges Liz was being helped into the inflatable with its powerful Mercury outboard engine. They swept out of the cove and along the coast towards Cala Flores. After about half a mile they pulled in shore to a totally secluded strip of gleaming sand no more than fifty yards wide with high overhanging black rocks on both sides giving shelter from the breeze and shade if the sun became too much. Tony jumped out of the boat and held out his hand to Liz who half tripped with her short legs having difficulty in climbing over the wide sides of the inflatable. But Tony held her firmly and only released her when she had regained her balance.

'*A las cinco, amigo. Hasta luego.*'

'*Perfecto, a las cinco,*' Paco replied. He smiled broadly.

'You have a good time, *senorita,*' he said to Liz who felt herself blushing furiously. She had always had this dream of making love on a deserted beach with a warm sea washing round her ankles and here she was with a complete stranger whom she had only met little more than an hour ago with her husband a mile or two inland probably just getting ready to play his second round of golf.

'Isn't this lovely?' she said nervously as she watched Paco's boat disappear round the headland, leaving them totally alone. 'I never knew there were little beaches like this along this bit of coast,' she added.

'Yes, it's gorgeous,' Tony replied. 'There are three or four of them of somewhat different sizes, but this one is my favourite and if Paco knows I'm coming he always saves this one for me and tells other people that its *privado*. He's a good friend. I've got some fruit and a bottle of white wine in the cold box. Would you like some?'

'Sounds wonderful,' she murmured, all thoughts of keeping off alcohol before sundown vanishing from her mind. Tony opened the box, removed a bottle of 'Blanc Pescador', deftly uncorked it and poured two glasses. He passed her one.

'Here's to the rest of your holiday, Liz,' he said. They clinked glasses.

'Suddenly I think it could be wonderful,' she said simply and drank deeply of the fresh dry white wine which came from the Gerona area of north eastern Spain. Tony went back to the cold box and when his hands reappeared he was holding a crescent of fresh juicy water melon, its dark pips glistening against the pink flesh. She took the melon and bit into it, the juice running down her chin, her neck and between her deep swelling breasts. Would Tony lick the juice from her body she thought if she really made a mess. She felt really randy. She closed her eyes the better to imagine what she most wanted him to do, her whole body aching for him and she could feel herself moistening between her thighs. She heard a splash, opened her eyes and there was Tony swimming strongly some twenty

13

yards away. She came out of her sensuous reverie suddenly. What had she been thinking of? Here she was, a forty-eight-year-old married woman, reasonably attractive and looking young for her age people said, but not in any sense a *femme fatale*. She had been married to Tom for twenty-four years, the children were virtually grown up with Jean getting married next year and Peter was in his first year at Cambridge. Tom, a successful chartered surveyor, hoped to retire in three or four years and whole new horizons were opening up for them when at last they would have the time and the money to have long holidays, go to the theatre more, eat at decent restaurants, buy good clothes that suited her and have her hair done regularly. She was crazy being here with Tony. With his reputation if Tom were to discover what she had done, let alone what she had just been fantasising about, there would be hell to pay. Yes, she must be sensible. It would have been fine, even wonderful for someone of Jean's age but she was a mature woman, not a romantic young girl.

Tony came walking up the beach from the edge of the Mediterranean which shimmered as far as the eye could see, not flat calm but with enough ripples to give it life. There were a few sailing boats in the distance while almost on the horizon some larger vessels ploughed along, probably going to Cartagena or even Gibraltar. Those going in the other direction might be on their way to Alicante or Palma.

Tony was well tanned, just under six feet tall, much less heavily built than Tom, with an unusually flat stomach for someone in his late forties. A small patch of hair on his chest glistened from the sea and another narrow strip of hair ran down from his waist and disappeared into his well-cut trunks which were not all revealing like the ones Peter wore ('Pays to advertise, Ma' he had said to her) but were shaped like boxer shorts.

14

'I needed that,' Tony said.

'Why?'

'Can I be totally honest?'

'I never like anyone to be anything else.'

'Well, I think it was the sight of the melon juice running down between your breasts. It just drove me wild and if I hadn't gone for a swim I think I would have grabbed you and tried to tear off your costume. You would have slapped my face and we would never have got to know each other, let alone become friends. As it is I hope we can talk, find out about each other and hopefully want to see each other again.'

Liz gave no indication that the last thing she would have dreamt of doing was slap his face or that she would probably have had his trunks off before he had undressed her but said:

'Thank you for being honest and for the compliment of being attracted to me, it doesn't happen very often nowadays and I, too, hope we can be friends. Tell me about yourself.'

She learnt that he had been a top amateur golfer, on the verge of the Walker Cup team, had turned pro and been on the professional tour for five years without achieving any real success. He had got married during that period but when his wife, June, had their first baby he had got a job as a teaching pro, first as an assistant at Aldburgh and then 15 years ago had landed the job as professional at Sheringham. He now made a fairly good living especially during the summer when lots of visitors came to the course and he had a good reputation as a teacher being retained by the Norfolk Golf Union to coach the junior county side.

Three years ago June had fallen for one of the club members and he was now divorced but still lived in what had been the matrimonial home. His elder son was in the

Army but his younger son was leaving school that summer and wanted to join Tony in the pro's shop. Tony didn't want him to turn pro so young as he felt he had the potential to go places in the amateur game and at 17 years of age this had not yet been tested.

They finished the melon and the wine and all too soon they heard the throb of the outboard and Paco came round the headland and headed for them. They picked up their things and climbed back into the inflatable, getting back to the cove in about five minutes. Tony paid Paco 1,000 pesetas and Liz never even thought of offering her share. Suddenly life was back to reality. Could she tell Tom about the afternoon, or indeed any part of it? Need he ever know? Would he believe that nothing had happened knowing Tony's reputation?

'Could you drop me off at the *supermercado* in Bellaluz?' she heard herself saying. 'There are one or two things I want for breakfast, and I'll walk back from there.'

'Are you sure?' Tony said. 'It's still pretty hot.'

'Yes, I'll be fine. I'd like the walk.' At least it will explain my absence she was thinking if Tom has got back early and there is less chance of my being recognised getting out of Tony's Porsche in Bellaluz than at Miradores. They pulled up in the car park behind the little supermarket and Tony squeezed her hand lightly.

' 'Til tomorrow then,' he said.

'Yes, I'll be there and thank you for a lovely afternoon – it was perfect.'

'I enjoyed it very much as well,' Tony said, slipping the car into gear and pulling away.

2

Liz's mind was in a whirl. Mechanically she bought some eggs and milk and a few slices of the rather disappointing Spanish bacon and set off back to the flat. What time was it? 5.35. What time had Tom said he would be back? Sixish. It was a quarter of an hour's walk back to the flat. 'Please God let me get back before Tom' she said to herself. 'Let me at least have time for a shower to wash away the sand and then I can work out what I'm going to say to him.' But another part of her was saying 'What the hell are you worried about? You've done nothing wrong, just had a few lecherous thoughts. Surely everyone is entitled to a few of those?' But she was married and she had gone out with another man. Not just another man but an attractive available man who had a reputation as a womaniser. No, Tom would not understand. He would have thought it most unreasonable if he had done something similar and Liz had not understood but that was another matter.

She remembered when he had played in the Evergreen Mixed Foursomes last year at Worplesdon and he had rung that first evening and said, 'Got through today, old girl but we've got an early start tomorrow so Margot and I thought we'd stay the night up here. There's quite a decent pub just down the road from the Club so, see you tomorrow. Miss you,' and put the phone down. Margot was just fifty and this was the first year she had been eligible to play in the Evergreens. She had been widowed the previous winter and openly admitted that she missed her sex life. But when Liz had asked if he had slept with her Tom had been wildly indignant.

'For God's sake woman! Can't you trust me? I'm a happily married man! I love you! You know that. We booked two single rooms – they were at opposite ends of the bloody pub. You can ask them yourself.' He picked up the phone and started dialling. 'Worplesdon Bridge Hotel – hold on a moment.' He passed the phone to Liz. 'Go on, ask them your bloody self as you obviously don't believe me.' Liz took the receiver and replaced it.

'Of course I believe you, I'm sorry darling.' That was the last time she had mentioned it but of course Tom would have booked two rooms but what did that prove? Tom always liked what he called a quickie before dinner and for a man in his mid-fifties was unusually rampant first thing in the morning.

'Nothing like a good screw followed by a cool shower to settle the swing. Helps the putting too. Makes you more relaxed.' He had often said this to her, especially if he had won a competition after that sort of a start to his day. 'You know, darling,' he had once said 'if we ever fall on hard times I'm going to be a pimp and hire you out during the Open. We could make a fortune.'

She approached the flat. No car outside. Her prayers had been answered. She unlocked the patio doors, hastily put the food in the fridge and climbed into the bath before undressing so that when she took her clothes off the sand would go into the bath and be washed away without leaving tell-tale signs on the bathroom floor. As she slipped out of her costume she could smell herself. She turned on the shower above the bath, sprayed vigorously between her thighs, rinsed her costume and began to relax. She threw the clothes she had just removed into the dirty linen basket in the corner of the bathroom and heard the patio doors open.

'That you darling?' she called. 'I'm in the shower – would you like to bring me a G & T?' Tom put his head round the door.

'Headache better then? God, you look wonderful. Stay there and I'll join you.'

In no time he was back with a large gin and tonic which he put down by the side of the bath, stepped out of his shorts, pulled off his socks and pants and climbed into the bath with her. He was just over a foot taller than her so that when he was standing up things didn't really seem to be in the right places. But he did a wonderful massage of her neck and shoulder muscles and she held her head against his chest with the warm water flowing over them. She could feel him grow against her, first pressing against her pubic hair and then as he grew stronger he stepped away and let his penis come vertically between them, the tip almost touching the bottom of her breasts. She bent her knees and cradled it in her hands squeezing it tenderly.

'What a big boy, you are,' she said and slowly, langorously she put out her tongue and licked him gently moving his foreskin backwards and forwards. She could feel him throbbing in her hands and against her tongue. She turned off the shower and taking Tom by the hand sat him on the bathroom stool. She put her right leg round his back and slowly lowered herself on to him carrying most of her weight on her left leg so that not all of him came inside her. Slowly she went up and down, each time letting a little more of him enter inside her while he kissed her nipples, first tenderly but getting rougher as more and more of her breasts disappeared inside his mouth. They both felt themselves building up to orgasm and with perfect timing as his sperm surged inside her she came with a long shuddering sigh. They clasped each other in silence for a minute or two while he gradually subsided inside her. Liz pulled her head back from behind his left ear.

'Not bad for a couple of old chaps,' she said.

'Bloody wonderful, old girl, it's really been a good day. Great sex. Gorgeous weather. Two wins at golf and a nice dinner to look forward to at La Tana.'

Liz got up and sat on the bidet while Tom got back under the shower. She was thinking furiously as the cool water cleansed her private parts and washed away Tom's semen. She must say something to Tom. He was in a good mood, that would help. If she didn't say something now it would be much more difficult later on or even impossible. She had always said that if you had committed some indiscretion, however minor, if you did not confess within the first half hour you never would and then you got involved in a web of lies and deceit. Besides, one of Tom's friends was bound to see her on the practice ground tomorrow.

'Tom, you know the golf pro who was on the balcony at lunchtime, Tony Seddon?'

'The womaniser, yes.'

'Well, I don't know about that. Anyway he was in the paper shop when I left and he gave me a lift to Bellaluz 'cos I wanted some things for breakfast. He asked me if I played golf and I said I'd never tried and he offered to give me a lesson tomorrow, just to see if I liked it. No charge and no obligation he said. You don't mind, do you?'

Tom stepped out of the bath and started towelling himself. He looked at Liz who was beginning to put on make-up in front of the bathroom mirror so that he could only see her reflection. He really wanted to see her reaction but it was difficult.

'Not in principle, in *principle* I'd be delighted if you took the game up but a lesson with Tony Seddon? Why can't I take you down to the practice ground and show you the rudiments?'

'But Tom, you like playing, you've got your regular games and good player though you are, you're not a trained teacher and your clubs would be much too big and heavy for me.' Liz was putting on mascara now so he could not see her eyes.

'Well, OK then but just the one lesson mind. I don't suppose even he could get up to much in one lesson on this practice ground. It's usually so bloody crowded with total wankers it's hard to find a place to hit a few balls in safety.' Tom paused. 'No, I'm being unreasonable. I've heard he is a first class teacher and if you can make love to me like that I don't think you're looking for anyone else.'

Liz turned round and smiled. 'Thank you, Tom. Life is just beginning for us – I wouldn't want to spoil that, would I?'

Part of her really believed that but she couldn't help remembering how she had felt on the beach and even while they had been making love, good though it had been, she had had a brief mental picture of Tony and she had wondered 'Could it feel like this with him or would it be even better?' And she tingled with expectation at the thought that tomorrow she would see Tony again.

'Is it the usual eight of us this evening?' she asked.

'Well, funnily enough it isn't. Tony Seddon is joining us. He came up when we were having a drink just now in the bar and said to Harold, "Look, I hate misunderstandings. If I said anything out of line to your wife a couple of years ago I apologise unreservedly. Can we let bygones be bygones and can I buy you all a drink?" Well, you know Harold, he's not the one to harbour a grudge so the upshot is Tony's joining us all for a drink and then coming on to La Tana. Maybe I'll tell him not to try anything on with you.'

'For God's sake Tom, I hope you don't. I'd be mortified. As you said yourself I'm sure he can find someone younger and more attractive than me and it would be suggesting he was attracted to me. Imagine how I'd feel if he said, "Well, actually Tom your wife doesn't turn me on at all, so she's quite safe." '

'I don't think he is so tactless that he'd say a thing like that, even if he thought it, which I doubt – still I see what you mean. Funny he didn't say anything about your lesson though.'

'Probably because I said I'd have to ask you first,' Liz lied.

'Anyway I can confirm our arrangement this evening. That's great.' Liz began to relax, she felt she had handled things quite well. Just as long as Tony didn't say anything about their trip to the beach (but he wouldn't, would he) perhaps she would be able to have a word with him quietly early on in the evening.

They started to get dressed. In some ways Liz found it easier in England where going out for a meal tended to be a relatively formal occasion. In Spain where everything was so informal it was easy to seem overdressed. She decided on a rather pretty white blouse with her turquoise trousers and matching shoes. Very simple but they made her feel good and people said the blue suited her and matched her eyes.

Tom, on the other hand loved eating out in Spain as he wore the same clothes for eating out, shopping or playing golf. His only concession to going out for a meal was a clean shirt and he'd probably wear the same one for golf the next day.

They finished their shared gin and tonic and strolled up to Harold and Margaret's flat which was only a couple of minutes walk. Dick and Sue were already there, Sue looking astonishingly brown considering she had only had four days in the sun, but she did tan easily and obviously didn't worry about skin cancer.

Harold poured them both his Spanish version of a Pimms. It was like an English Pimms except that he used Spanish sparkling wine instead of lemonade and one was great but two were lethal. Just then Gilbert, Jane and Tony arrived together, Jane looking flushed having only left the tennis club about half an hour before and Tony looked devastating in a blue safari suit which was immaculately pressed and somehow accentuated his lean figure.

Harold said, 'I think you know just about everyone don't you, Tony, except perhaps Liz, Tom's wife?' but Liz interrupted.

'Actually we met this afternoon. Tony kindly gave me a lift to Bellaluz and he's going to give me a golf lesson tomorrow.' She flashed a smile at Tony. 'That's still OK is it?' Tony smiled back and his eyes showed understanding of what she had said and not said.

'Yes, if ten o'clock is all right for you. I've got another lesson at eleven but an hour is quite long enough for a first effort. Did you manage to get a lift back from Bellaluz? I felt awful leaving you there but I was meeting someone at the cove, and I was a little late as it was.'

'No, I walked. It's not really very far.'

How clever of him to have mentioned the cove, perhaps in case his car had been seen there. Dick and Jane had a Pimms but Tony asked for a soft drink.

'I don't want to be a killjoy,' he said. 'but the *Guardia* seem quite interested in my car so if I'm going off the complex I limit myself to a couple of glasses of wine with my meal.'

'Very sensible,' Liz said. 'I wish Tom did the same but although he's quite responsible at home he seems to forget all about breathalysers in Spain so it is usually one of us girls – I use the word loosely – who ends up driving home.'

They all chatted together easily over their drinks. It was good Tony being there as the conversation was much more wide ranging with subjects being discussed which rarely got an airing among the eight of them.

'Good heavens,' said Harold. 'It's a quarter to nine and I booked the table for nine. We'd better be on our way. Whose cars are we taking?'

'I'm very happy to take mine,' said Tony, 'but I'm afraid I can only take one passenger.'

Liz wanted to take one step smartly forward but resisted the impulse, and Tom said: 'Is that your 944? I've hankered after one for ages and now the kids are off our hands may indulge myself soon. Is it OK if I come with you?'

'Of course, delighted. You can have a drive sometime if you like but not after two and a half Pimms.'

Tom and Tony left and Liz went with Harold and Margaret in their hired Seat while Dick and Sue went with Gilbert and Jane in its twin. Liz was pleased to share the car with Harold and Margaret as it gave her a chance to ask Margaret about Tony two years ago.

'What was all this business at lunchtime about Tony and you, Margaret?' she asked as they drove towards the strip.

'No idea,' said Margaret, 'I wasn't there. What business anyway?'

Harold interjected. 'I just said how I'd given him a flea in his ear because he was coming it a bit strong with you and I've heard he's quite a ladies' man.'

'Oh that,' said Margaret laughing. 'We were all a bit tiddly that evening – I think we'd been at the Pimms again – and if anything I was the one you should have given a flea in the ear. I'm sure I made more advances than Tony.

Don't worry Liz. I'm sure you'll be quite safe on the practice ground.'

'That's funny, that's exactly what Tom said. Where wouldn't I be safe I wonder?'

'If you ever find out do let me know,' said Margaret archly. 'You've got to admit he is a bit of a dish.'

They pulled up in the street by the side of La Tana, a speciality fish restaurant, from where they could see and hear the Mediterranean lapping against the harbour walls of Cabo de Palos and smell the fishermen's nets which were stretched out on the quay to dry.

'Well, I know one thing,' Harold said to Margaret, 'you are not sitting next to this dish, as you call him, at dinner. You've had Pimms again and I'm not going to spoil my meal wondering if you're playing footsie under the table.' They all laughed and entered the restaurant. Tom and Tony were already there and Tom was obviously planning the seating. He had put Tony at one end with Sue and Jane on either side of him and Liz was between Dick and Harold on one side while Margaret was between Gilbert and Tom on the other. Was it just coincidence that Tom had got her and Margaret away from Tony, Liz wondered.

La Tana was one of their favourite restaurants with enough noise and local clientele to create a real Spanish atmosphere.

El patron only spoke as much English as was necessary when serving English guests and seemed very happy to cope with Tom's pidgin Spanish. Tom always seemed to take control of the ordering on these occasions and Tony did not attempt to usurp his authority although Liz knew he spoke Spanish fluently. The majority of them wanted the fresh sea bass and *el patron* brought in a fine fish of suitable size to show them before it was cooked. Liz had hers grilled with garlic and their speciality side salad with

25

lots of the greeny orange tomatoes, red and green peppers and olives. Harold, of course, had steak, but then he always did.

Conversation flowed easily and Liz noticed that Tony seemed to be amusing Sue and Jane and obviously knew enough about tennis to discuss results around the world and who might win Wimbledon this year. At the end of the meal they had obviously spent enough to merit a glass each of *Melocoton*, the delicious peach liqueur which was always served ice cold in a frosted glass with the compliments of the house and Liz wondered why this never seemed to happen in England. An appreciation of one's custom did not cost a lot but one went away with a warm glow, not just alcohol induced, which made one want to come again.

The men were arguing about how to divide the bill with Tony offering to pay one fifth but the others saying they had invited him and in any case why should he pay more than one ninth. It was all rather petty but eventually some compromise was reached. Liz wondered how they would travel back but again Tom took control.

'No need for you to worry about us, old boy. We've got two cars and we all live past the Hotel. Thanks for joining us and I'll be interested to hear if you think Liz has got any talent. See you tomorrow, I expect.' Tony did not argue but shook each lady's hand, (was that little squeeze just for her, Liz wondered, or did they all get that?) said how much he had enjoyed the evening and slid behind the wheel of his Porsche which growled off towards the main road.

The rest of them decided this was not an evening when they wanted more drinks or to go dancing or gambling at the casino about four miles further down the strip so Tom joined Liz, Harold and Margaret and they all went to their respective apartments.

Tom was playing in the weekly medal next day and was first off at 8.44. He had also arranged to play another nine holes with his pals at four o'clock so it was going to be another full day. When they got back to Miradores Liz asked Margaret if she could help clear up but Margaret said she would do it tomorrow as she had a free morning and just wanted to go to bed.

They said goodnight and Tom and Liz carried on to their flat. Tom walked straight up the stairs to the bathroom, cleaned his teeth, undressed and was fast asleep by the time Liz had put a few things out for breakfast and emptied the ashtrays. As she did not feel sleepy she poured herself a small *Cuarenta y tres*, a sweet Spanish liqueur made locally at Cartagena, and took it out on to the patio.

She loved sitting on the patio late at night when it was totally quiet apart from the odd car driving along the road below and what she could only describe as the night sounds of La Manga, a sort of combination of crickets and the frogs by the lakes on the golf course. Quite different sounds from anything one heard in England but she knew that if she could be transported to La Manga by some supernatural means in the middle of the night she would always identify it correctly by these unique noises. She sipped her drink and leant back in the patio chair, her eyes half closed. What a day it had been! How could Tony have set her heart racing the way it had and induced more lustful thoughts than she had experienced in twenty-four years of marriage?

She had never been unfaithful to Tom – a bit of petting in darkened rooms at Round Table parties some years back but she had never enjoyed it and sometimes wondered if some of the men who had fondled her breasts or tried to put their hands up her skirt had done these things out of habit or because they thought it was a form of

27

flattery, rather than a genuine desire. On balance she thought it was probably experimentation as undoubtedly a few of the Ladies Circlers seemed to enjoy it and some pretty heavy petting had gone on at these parties in the late sixties and early seventies. She didn't know of any full-blooded extra marital affair in Tom's Table but there had been the odd divorce amongst other Tablers and Circlers.

What was tomorrow going to bring? Obviously nothing on the practice ground but might Tony suggest another meeting? If he did what would she say? Her body knew the answer, she could tell as her nipples hardened and again she could feel herself moisten between her thighs. But she must be sensible, or did she mean careful. Tom was OK. As marriages go they both thought it was pretty good and a lot better than many of their friends had. Tom was selfish and very rarely made sacrifices to do what she wanted but then he worked hard and had a demanding job. And he did not object if she did her own thing with a girlfriend – in fact he encouraged her to do so saying it was only fair with the amount of golf he played and next year he was going to be Chairman of his branch of the Royal Institution of Chartered Surveyors and that was going to involve a lot of evening committee meetings and dinners, most of which would be stag affairs. She was already making plans for theatre visits and perhaps an evening class or two. Perhaps she would learn Spanish. And she was so looking forward to Jean's wedding. Tom would really push the boat out. She liked Chris, her fiancé, and she would have a really nice dress and everyone would say lovely things. She mustn't do anything that could prejudice her being with Tom for that. Besides they had a nice house which they had just about got as they wanted. Tom might not be over generous but neither did he keep her short of money. He did not beat her. They had sex pretty regularly and it was good sex. She could not remember the last time she had not achieved orgasm and many of her friends thought this was amazing.

No, she must not be silly. She had far too much to lose. Still that lean tanned body and blue eyes haunted her and she wondered how strong she would be if Tony suggested another meeting. She finished her drink and went upstairs to bed snuggling up against Tom as she always did, either with his bottom against her stomach or sometimes the other way round. She closed her eyes and could see the little sandy beach where she had been that afternoon, but centre stage was Tony, coming out of the water which sparkled like diamonds on his hair.

3

The alarm went off at ten to eight and there was the usual panic while Tom showered, shaved, got dressed, and wolfed his breakfast before walking down to the golf club in time for his 8.44 start. Liz often wondered why he did not set the alarm earlier or ask for a later starting time but it was normal at La Manga for competitors to go out in handicap order and Tom liked to play with people of comparable standard in the competitions and not with wankers, tossers, hand jobs or whatever his in-word of the week was at the time.

Tom looked at his watch. 'Christ, 8.25,' he said and dashed upstairs to clean his teeth and pay his mandatory after breakfast visit to the loo. By 8.30 he was down again picking up his golf clubs and shoes. 'Bye luv. Be interested to hear how the lesson goes. No hanky panky, mind!'

'Of course not, darling – hope you win. I'll be at the 37th at about one and will tell you all about it.'

Tom left the flat and Liz poured herself a second cup of coffee. No panic for her. Still more than an hour and a quarter before she was due on the practice ground. She finished her coffee, washed up the breakfast things and swept the tiled floors of the living room and patio. She then went upstairs, had a leisurely shower, put on a minimum amount of make-up and decided she would wear a lemon tee-shirt with matching Bermuda shorts. It was a flattering colour and made her look more tanned than she really was. 'Shoes' she thought 'What the hell do I do for shoes?' She had got some trainers at home but that wasn't much use as she had not brought them with her. Had she got time to buy some golf shoes? No, that was crazy. This might be the one and only golf lesson of her life, although she hoped not. No, the low heeled sandals would have to do or she could play in bare feet.

The time was 9.45 – just right, so she went up to the car park and drove down to the Club. She walked down to the practice ground where she could see Tony at the far end with a tall slim blond young man who was hitting the ball what seemed like miles and she wondered why anyone who could hit the ball like that would want a lesson. Tony waved to her and as she approached said to the young man, 'Just weaken your grip slightly with your right hand and hit a couple more.' Again two balls went off like rifle shots. 'That's good. See you tomorrow at the same time, Per.' The young Swede picked up his clubs and gave Liz a quizzical look. 'OK Tony. Thanks.' He said with barely a trace of an accent.

Tony smiled at Liz as Per walked away. 'That boy, Per Sandstrom, is only fifteen but he's down to one handicap already and I think he could really make it in a few years' time. Very dedicated people, the Swedes. Anyway enough of that. I'm glad you came, Liz, I was worried you might change your mind. How are you today? You look very nice I must say.'

'I'm fine – I'm nervous – I haven't got any golf shoes and watching the boy hit shots like that makes me feel even worse,' Liz said.

'Don't worry. Per is one in a million but he didn't start like that. Just look around you, you can't say everyone down here is brilliant.' Liz looked round and saw a

31

woman of about the same age as her hit a ball about five yards and completely miss the next one.

'Maybe I could be as good as her.'

Tony smiled. 'She hasn't been to me for a lesson. After one hour with me you'll be much better than that. The shoes don't matter today. You could play barefoot if you like, but if you decide to carry on, as I hope you will, you'll have to get some. They are not very expensive, even here. Now then down to business. I'm unusual among golf pros as I don't teach beginners to use a full swing until their confidence develops. The most important fundamental in a golf swing is keeping one's eye on the ball and one's head still and the reason most people move their head is that they are worried about where the ball is going, so I start with the grip and the stance and then I will get you to hit a few balls with a very short swing. That part of the swing, which is called the hitting area, is the most important part and if we get that right the rest will follow.'

'I've often heard Tom talk about the hitting area. Is it Eamon D'Arcy that Tom says has an awful swing but is good in the hitting area?'

'Yes, probably. He is a classic case but it's true of quite a few pros to a greater or less extent, but let's get back to you.' He showed her how to grip the club – not too tightly and with an interlocking grip as she had small hands; how to stand to the ball with knees slightly bent and with her arms fairly straight but not tense. He did not go on to the pivot, that would come later when she started a fuller swing, and a back swing no more than waist high but with a slight break in the wrists. He gave her a five iron and she started hitting balls. Sometimes she hit behind the ball and sometimes she topped it and on these occasions the ball only went a few yards but she never missed it and her best shots were going fifty or sixty yards. Tony encouraged her and complimented her whenever possible

32

and it seemed no time before a middle-aged couple, whom she had seen on the complex several times, arrived for their eleven o'clock lesson.

Liz felt quite elated in that she thought the golf lesson had gone well but for a whole hour Tony had not touched her, except to change her grip or the way she was standing to the ball and had said nothing romantic or suggested another meeting and now here were this other couple. . . . She was about to say 'Could we arrange another lesson?' when Tony reached into his pocket and pulled out a card which he handed to her. 'That's where to reach me if you would like to fix up another lesson. That was very promising for a first time so I hope you will. Bye.'

'Y-y-yes, thank you,' Liz stammered, 'I'm sure I will,' and walked away. She looked at the card. It said Tony Seddon, Golf Professional, Sheringham Golf Club and a couple of telephone numbers. She turned it over. There was a handwritten note. I'm in room 216 at the Hotel. I'll be there at four and I hope you will too. She felt a sharp jolt in her stomach and felt herself go weak at the knees. She half staggered before regaining her composure and thrust the card in the pocket of her shorts. She looked back towards Tony but he had his back to her and was giving all his attention to the middle-aged couple.

'What a nerve the man's got' she thought. He must have written the note before he had even given her the lesson, before he even knew that she was going to turn up and he had spent an hour with her as if she were a complete stranger and all the time he had this in mind. But what was this? Did he know Tom was playing golf at four? Had it been mentioned last night? She couldn't remember but she knew she would have to be there at four if only to tell him what an incredible nerve he had got and why couldn't he ask her straight out like any normal person. For a whole hour he could have asked her if she would come to his room and she could have said no or prevaricated but as it was she had this card burning a hole in her pocket and it must be destroyed as soon as possible. She went to the locker room and went into one of the loos. She re-read the note as if she could ever forget 'Room 216, 4pm.' She tore the card into minute pieces and flushed them down the loo waiting to see if all the pieces had disappeared. They seemed to have but just to make sure she waited for the cistern to refill and flushed it again.

Her heart was still pounding as she walked to the car and drove to Bellaluz to get some fresh bread and pâté for lunch. She and Tom usually had a snack lunch after Tom's mandatory three or four beers which followed his golf. She went back to the flat thinking she would have an hour with her book before going back to the Club at one to meet Tom, but her mind was in a whirl and she found herself reading and re-reading every page three or four times. She never thought she would not be in room 216 at four o'clock but what would she have said if she had been asked in a conventional way after her long self-examination on that same patio the night before.

She went up to the bathroom, made up her face and drove back to the Club to find Tom was already in the bar. He got up from his chair and pecked her on the cheek.

'This is Mike,' he said, 'and this is Nigel, a real bloody bandit, off seven. My wife Liz. What will you have, luv? The usual?'

'Yes please, Tom, that would be lovely.'

She sat down with the other two men while Tom went to the bar to get her *agua con gas*.

'Do I gather Tom didn't do very well?' she said.

'Well he played OK from tee to green but his putting let him down,' Mike replied, 'but Nigel here would have taken a lot of beating with a net 67. I understand you've been having a lesson this morning. How did it go?'

Tom returned with the drink.

'Mike was just asking me how my lesson went, darling,' Liz said. 'Pretty well I think. Tony seems a wonderful teacher. He really builds up your confidence and towards the end I felt I was hitting the ball fairly well.' She raised her glass to her lips.

'Cheers and thank you.'

'That's great,' said Tom. 'It would make our retirement if you played golf as well. Have you fixed up another lesson?'

'No, not yet but I'd like to in a day or two if that's all right. The only thing is, Tony says I must get some golf shoes. Can we afford it?'

'I don't think it will quite break the bank. You carry on. Apparently Tony taught Mike's wife and she's got down to twenty in a couple of years. Mind you she must be a few years younger than you,' Tom added hurtfully. 'Perhaps I'd better go to him for a putting lesson. I was hopeless this morning. Three putted five times, once from about ten feet.'

Just then Tony came in and Liz hoped he would join them but he waved, smiled and went over to the middle-aged couple he had been teaching earlier. They had another couple of drinks and then went up to the flat for their lunch.

'No hanky panky or secret assignations with lover boy, then?' Tom said.

'Don't be stupid, Tom,' Liz said sharply. 'If your mother had heard every word spoken between us this morning even she could not have taken exception and she can read an innuendo into Hello.'

'OK, luv – sorry, can I help get lunch ready? I'm starving.'

'No, there's really nothing to do but you could pour me a glass of wine if you'd like to do that. I'll pop if I have any more fizzy water.'

He went over to the shelf and poured a glass of Jumilla Tinto from the two litre flagon they filled every few days at the Bodega in El Algar. It only cost 85 pesetas a litre, but tasted just as good as conventionally bottled wines at three or four times the price.

Liz carried the french bread, butter, pâté, olives from the market at Cabo de Palos and fruit out to the patio where Tom was already sitting down looking at the sports results in yesterday's *Telegraph*. He looked up from the paper. 'That looks good. Have you got any plans for the afternoon?'

'No, not really, you know me, I'm always happy reading and I think I'm going to really enjoy my new Mary Wesley.'

'Oh, good,' Tom said, cutting the bread and helping himself to the butter, which was already beginning to melt under the midday sun. 'I think I'll have half an hour on the putting green before going out if you don't mind. If I don't sort that out this holiday could cost a fortune.'

'Yes, that's fine,' said Liz, relieved that he would be leaving the flat a little bit earlier. 'Can I have the crossword bit of the paper if you're not wanting it?'

Tom separated the outside of the paper and passed it over and they finished the meal in silence with Liz looking at the crossword and Tom reading the financial news after he had finished the sports section.

'Shall I make some coffee?' Tom said suddenly. 'Or do you want some more wine?'

'No, coffee would be lovely,' Liz said. 'Any idea what "Could be described in a ruder tale" could be? You read more dirty books than I do, it's nine letters with second letter "d" '.

Tom went through to the kitchen area of the living room and put on the filter machine, remembering that Spanish coffee was much stronger than the coffee they bought in England and neither of them liked it particularly strong.

'What about adulterer? Isn't it an anagram of ruder tale?' Liz felt a jolt in the pit of her stomach and involuntarily caught her breath.

'Y-Yes, that's it,' she said. 'Aren't you clever?'

Why couldn't she have asked Tom any other clue than that? She had better ask him another one quickly.

'What about "Relied on in hell but not elsewhere", eight letters, fourth letter "t" and penultimate letter "s"?'

'Must have "dis" in it somewhere,' Tom said. 'Yes, it's got to be distrust. Thought you'd have got that.'

This is ridiculous Liz thought. She put the paper down and began gathering up the lunch things and then took them through to the kitchen. She washed the plates before putting them in the enclosed rack above the draining board. It was such a good idea to have a plate rack in this position she always thought but she had never come across the same idea in England. The coffee was now ready and she poured two cups and took them out to the patio. They drank it in silence before Tom looked at his watch.

'Right, think I'll be off – good job you know where I am or you might distrust me and think I was an adulterer. Or perhaps its you that I should distrust.' He added almost as an afterthought. 'OK if I take the car?'

Liz was glad he had not waited for a reply to his first suggestion. 'Yes, that's fine. I may go down to the hotel sometime to confirm our flight but I'm not ready yet and I'd like the walk.'

What a brilliant idea that was she thought: a reason for being at the Hotel and for some reason it was always her that did that sort of chore although Tom passed the hotel about four times a day.

'Right, see you then. I'll be back by seven.' Tom walked to the car.

Liz looked at her watch – 3.20. 'I think I'll have a quick shower,' she thought. She went up to the bathroom and relished the sensuous feeling of the warm water flowing down her body. She powdered her parts and her breasts with Chanel talc she saved for special occasions without it really crossing her mind to use her normal Boots variety. Then she chose her prettiest underwear, the Janet Rega panties and matching lacy bra under a white silk blouse and black lawn skirt. She looked at herself in the mirror – she looked great but it was only twenty to four. Nobody dressed like that at twenty to four at La Manga. She would stand out like a lighthouse. She removed the blouse and skirt and replaced them with a Lacoste T shirt and white denim skirt. That was better, she thought. A dab of perfume, Chanel of course, to go with the talc, and she picked up her handbag and set off for the Hotel. The Falcon Travel rep was in the foyer and she went up to him and confirmed the flight for herself and Tom. She looked at postcards for a moment or two as she felt everyone was watching her and then quickly walked down the stairs to the landing which gave access to the bedrooms. There was the sign '201–220'. She walked on, praying that she was not going to see anyone she knew and wondering what on earth to say if she did, but luck was with her – there was no one but she'd still have to walk back. This was crazy. Why was she doing it? She was outside 215. She could still turn back. She must turn back. She could ring Tony and make it clear that she was not the sort of woman who went to men's hotel bedrooms in the middle of the afternoon, or any other time come to that. She would tell him what a cheek he had to even suggest it but still her feet were taking her inexorably towards 216. She was outside the door. She half raised her hand to knock. No, she wouldn't do it. She couldn't understand how she had got this far. She turned to walk back to the foyer but who was coming down the passage but Tony. He ran towards her.

'I'm so sorry, Liz – I got held up – its inexcusable.' He had his key in the door and half pushed her into his room.

'B-b-but,' she stammered.

'No buts,' he said. 'You look wonderful and I'm all hot and sticky. I'm going to pour you a glass of wine, unless you'd prefer a soft drink, you're going to sit down in the chair over there while I have a very quick shower and I'll be with you in a jiffy.'

'A glass of wine would be lovely,' Liz said and sat down in the easy chair by the window. He got a bottle of Vin Sol from the fridge and poured two glasses.

'You look and smell so clean and fresh the least I can do is have a shower, but if we'd both arrived hot and sweaty I'd have suggested a shower afterwards,' he said smiling wickedly. He handed her a glass which was misting slightly from the chill of the wine.

'Don't go away,' he said and disappeared into the bathroom. She could hear the shower gushing away as she looked around the room. It was quite small and sparsely furnished but with a good sized fitted cupboard with built-in dressing table in the centre and what the Spanish called a *cama matrimonial*. When she and Tom had gone to buy a double bed in Cartagena they had asked for a *cama doble* to be met with a puzzled expression before being shown some bunk beds. She had always thought the Spanish words were rather nice and implied a morality which certainly no longer applied in Spain if even half what she had heard was true about what happened on the Strip, especially during the summer holiday season. The water stopped.

'What did you mean by "afterwards?" ' Liz called out.

Tony put his head round the bathroom door, dripping

slightly. 'Afterwards? Well after we have got to know each other better,' he said, smiling enigmatically. His head disappeared and he came out of the bathroom a moment or two later wearing a white towelling robe which came down to just above his knees. It was pretty obvious that was all he was wearing Liz thought and at the sight of him she could feel her resolution waning.

'I was on my way home when you came along just now. I don't think this is sensible at all. In fact I don't know why I'm still here.' Tony walked over to her chair and knelt in front of her. He took her head in his hands and gently kissed her on the lips. He picked up her hands and gently kissed them on the backs before turning them over and kissing them harder on the palms. He leant back on his haunches still holding her hands gently and looked her straight in the eyes.

'Of course it's not sensible and of course you must go if you really want to but you know I find you very attractive and you must feel something for me to be here at all and if we are going to get to know each other better there is probably no safer place in the whole of La Manga than here in the hotel while Tom is playing golf.'

He let go of her hands and removed her sandals, gently caressing her feet and calves but stopping at her knees. He kissed her toes one by one, first the left foot and then the right. She closed her eyes. This was so relaxing. It all felt so right. She leant forward and caressed the back of his neck, first gently and then harder running her fingers down close to his spine and then wider along the back of his shoulders.

'Mm, you could do that all day,' he said. 'It's fantastic.'

He pushed her skirt up and started kissing the inside of her legs above her knees while she continued to massage his shoulders and neck.

'I mustn't crease your skirt,' he said and got to his feet

40

pulling her up from her chair. He kissed her again on the lips, the first time they had kissed with open mouths. Their tongues met and explored each other's mouths, tasting each other for the first time and liking what they found. Tony pulled her shirt out from her skirt and drew it up over her head. He kissed her neck and ears while undoing her bra. His robe fell open and he pressed her against him, her erect nipples against his chest. He undid the zip of her skirt and it fell to the floor. He knelt down again his lips brushing her breasts, her stomach and then her pubic hair as he gently pulled her panties down over her bottom. He stood up slowly brushing the same parts of her body with his lips but in reverse order and she could feel his penis pressing hard against her. They half walked, half hobbled towards the bed with their arms wrapped tightly round each other. The backs of Liz's legs came to the side of the divan and she fell backwards with Tony on top of her. She felt aflame with desire. She parted her legs wanting to take Tony inside her and to entwine her legs around his back and hold him there forever.

'Not yet,' Tony murmured gently. 'It would be all over in seconds the way we feel right now.' He pulled away from her. 'We must explore each other's bodies first. I want to kiss every part of you, taste every part of you, inside and out. Shall I start at the top and work down or would you prefer the other way round?' Without waiting for an answer he kissed her hair, her forehead, her eyes, her ears exploring them with his tongue and making her shiver despite the heat of the afternoon, her nose, her mouth, her neck with gentle nibbles but not hard enough to cause a love bite, her shoulders, her nipples and then opening his mouth wide taking most of each of her breasts into his mouth in turn, her arms pressing his lips hard against the inside of her elbows, her stomach causing small cramps of excitement and down to her pubic hair,

41

the inside of her thighs, her knees, her calves, her feet and then working upwards but this time with her legs apart.

When he reached her vagina he parted her pubic hair with his fingers and then gently the lips. 'Gorgeous,' he murmured as he slipped his hands under her bottom and she put her legs over his shoulders. Initially he caressed her clitoris with his tongue gently from side to side, up and down, down and up – Liz had her eyes closed rejoicing in the untold pleasure he was giving her. 'More, more,' she said pressing herself hard against his mouth. He plunged his tongue inside her and she came at once.

'Told you,' he said but he didn't stop and carried on caressing her bottom with his hands and exploring her vagina with his tongue. This is such bliss she thought. Why is it that oral sex becomes so rare when one is married? She could feel herself building up to another climax which seemed to affect her whole body and she could feel her vagina awash with her own juices and Tony's saliva. He removed his head from between her legs and lay alongside her gently kissing her face and hair while she lay totally relaxed in his arms.

'That was just wonderful,' Liz said. 'Are you sure you're only a golf pro, or do you give sex lessons as well? It's your turn now. Something similar would you say?'

'Sounds good to me,' Tony replied.

She moved him on to his back and sat astride him while she kissed him from head to toe leaving a trail of her juices down his body. Like Tony she wanted to leave the best till last and only brushed his penis, which was lying flat on his stomach and only slightly enlarged, with her lips on the way down to his legs and feet. As she came up again she let her breasts fall one each side of his penis and slowly moved upwards and downwards with her nipples rubbing against Tony's stomach giving him slight jolts also. Almost immediately she could feel his penis grow and

42

become stiff but she continued up and down, up and down watching Tony's face, his lips half parted and eyes closed but with an expression of deep contentment.

She then took his penis in her hands and grasped it tightly, pulling back the foreskin slightly so that she could caress its pink tip with her tongue round and round and side to side and she could feel it beginning to throb in her hands while she squeezed it gently. Half of her wanted to plunge it deep inside her vagina and half wanted to feel him explode in her mouth and taste his semen. She pulled his foreskin back a little more and took him in her mouth still squeezing him gently in her hands while rubbing the end against her tongue and teeth until with an involuntary cry he came and she felt his semen burst into her mouth in three or four shuddering spasms. His whole body relaxed and she felt his penis become softer as the blood drained out of it. She let it fall out of her mouth and kissed his balls gently before lying down beside him.

'You're wonderful,' Tony said, 'you may need golf lessons but I don't believe you could improve your fellatio, that's for sure. Next time we might try adultery. What do you think?'

'I have to say there's nothing I would like better but opportunities may be hard to find. Remember we leave here in five days time and Tom doesn't always play golf in the afternoon. When can I have another golf lesson? At least we can see each other.'

'Tomorrow at about twelve would be fine for me.'

'Great, I'll try and find out Tom's plans for the rest of the holiday. Oh, Tony, I want you so much – to feel you inside me. Mmm, bliss. What's the time?'

Tony rolled over and picked up his watch from the bedside table. 'Five thirty.'

'My God,' Liz said. 'Tom will be finishing his golf any minute. Can I use your shower?'

Without waiting for an answer she rushed into the bathroom, turned on the shower and sprayed herself vigorously between her legs and in her mouth. This is horrible she thought. It had been so wonderful and here she was trying to remove all traces of Tony. She would have liked to stay in his arms with their sweat and juices intermingling and talk about what they had done, what they had liked best, where they went from now and then after an hour or so . . . and then a leisurely shower, dinner and then. . . . She got out of the shower, towelled herself dry, rubbed some of Tony's toothpaste against her front teeth and gums and came back into the bedroom. Tony had not moved, he still lay there with eyes half closed.

'An hour or two just isn't enough is it? See if there is anything you can do so that we can have longer together.'

Liz dressed, combed her hair, dabbed on some perfume and went over to the bed. She bent over, kissed Tony tenderly on the lips, and picking up his penis kissed that gently.

'Bye, big boy,' she said and walked to the door. 'Till twelve tomorrow.'

She walked up the passage towards reception with her mind in a turmoil. It had been so wonderful, probably the best sex she had ever had even though she had not held him inside her. But this was so horrible. She felt like a criminal on the run, every sound making her nervous and worried who might be round every corner. She walked up the steps to reception tentatively not wanting to be seen coming up from the bedroom area of the hotel by anyone she knew. It seemed clear. She walked over to the Falcon Travel desk.

'Hello, again,' she said. 'A friend of mine was wondering if there were any spare seats for tomorrow's flight.'

The rep looked up from his desk.

'Hello, Mrs Waldren. Yes, I think there are a couple

still, but coming back could be tricky. Ask your friend to come and see me as soon as possible and I'll see what I can sort out.'

'Thanks, thanks very much, I will. Bye.'

Liz looked at the clock above the reception desk. Five to six. She walked to the door of the hotel. Should she go straight back to the flat or see if Tom was in the bar? The bar was probably best she thought. She was remembering the last conversation she had with Tom and didn't want to go back to that on a one to one basis. No, much better to be in a group and then after a few drinks things would be easier and she might feel more normal, more relaxed, think more clearly even. But could she face Tom, even in a group, with the taste of Tony still in her mouth and her skin still glowing from his physical contact. No, better to walk a little and try and analyse her thoughts and emotions. In a half daze she walked up through the car park and along the road towards the tennis club.

4

Automatically she turned left at the exit from the car park but she was not thinking where she was going. She was not clear how she felt about Tony. Undoubtedly she longed for his touch, his body, his all over physical contact in a way she had never felt before about anyone but then he was a brilliant lover. The best she had ever known. Tom had not been experienced when they got married – not a virgin either but clumsy and quick and they had learned gradually from their mistakes, from novels, from *Cosmopolitan*-type magazines and generally from the greater freedom and explicitness that now existed in all matters connected with sex, whether in conversation, television or cinema.

Did she feel guilty? Strangely enough, she didn't. Would she feel guilty if they were found out? Probably. Did she want to leave Tom? Certainly not, they were used to each other. They were comfortable together. They had lots of mutual friends and she wouldn't want them having to decide with which one of them they would remain friendly which she had seen happen so often in other marriage break-ups. What would Tom do if he did find out? God knows but probably throw a monumental scene, walk out and come back a week or so later. He would certainly come back if he didn't have someone else to go to, and she didn't think he had. He could not live without having his meals cooked and his washing and ironing done for long.

So what were her feelings for Tony? Were they entirely physical? Did she know him well enough to judge? Not really. She had spent about ten hours in his company, four of those in a group when she had hardly talked to him at all, an hour learning golf when nothing personal had been said and two hours just now when they had been much too busy with their mouths and tongues to talk at all. Really it was only the few hours on the beach when they had talked and found out anything about each other. So, she was in lust with Tony. But love sometimes grew from lust, certainly more often than the other way round. She must talk to Tony about it. Suddenly the golf lessons did not seem important. What she most wanted to was talk to Tony, at least to start with. What were his feelings? Was she just another middle-aged woman who had fallen for his good looks and charm, to be instantly forgotten when she flew out from San Javier next week? Or did he have some special feeling for her as she had for him? She hoped so and he had certainly enjoyed his fellatio.

She was thinking better now. They were in lust. It wouldn't escalate to anything more but making love like that was amazing and she deserved a treat or two. After all she was sure Tom had been unfaithful a few times but she hadn't dug too deep because what would it really achieve? Better not to know for certain than feel threatened, so why shouldn't she have a little fling before it was too late? She turned into the tennis club. Jane was bound to be there. She could have a drink with her to explain her absence from the flat if Tom got back early. This was awful. Alibis seemed to be becoming second nature as if she did this sort of thing all the time and yet she had never done anything like it before. She walked up the steps to the balcony of the

47

tennis club. Sure enough Jane was there with three other people. Jane saw her immediately and waved.

'Hi, Liz. Come and join us. Would you like a drink?'

'Hello Jane, I thought you might be here. Yes, thanks. A glass of white wine would be nice. Have you had a good game?'

'Yes, super. Do you know my friend James, and this is Hans and Rika? This is Liz.'

James raised an arm in acknowledgement. Hans stood up, half bowed and clicked his heels except they didn't click as he was wearing tennis shoes and sat down again while Rika shook hands gravely.

'You play tennis too?' she said.

'No, I'm afraid not. I'm really very unathletic. I gave up when the children were about eleven and started beating me.'

The waiter brought over her glass of wine and put a chit for 110 pasetas on the table on top of a pile of several others. Perhaps Jane doesn't play as much tennis as I thought mused Liz. She had put her flush down to running round the court but maybe the *ginebras con tonicas* had more to do with it.

'Hey, didn't you have your golf lesson this morning with lover boy?' Jane asked. 'That's not unathletic. Did he put his arms around you to show you how to swing at the same time whispering sweet nothings into your shell like?'

Liz laughed easily as the golf lesson had, in fact, been so formal.

'No, nothing like that – but I enjoyed the lesson and certainly hit the ball better than I expected. I'm hoping to have another tomorrow or the next day if Tom doesn't mind. I don't think he will as he would really like me to take up golf.'

'Probably so he doesn't feel guilty playing as much as he does,' Jane replied. 'That's where Gilbert is lucky as he knows I'm happy playing tennis and although he plays occasionally he much prefers his golf.'

'One for the road, Jane?' said James.

'What a nice idea,' replied Jane, 'And then I really must get back to the flat. See if I can get back before Gilbert for a change.' Hans and Rika refused a drink and got up to leave.

'We play again tomorrow – 3.30 on clay?' Hans said.

'You bet,' Jane replied. 'You've got no chance tomorrow. I've got a lesson with Lorenzo in the morning and you'll think you're playing Steffi Graf. *Hasta la vista.*'

Again Hans clicked his heels, bowed gravely to the three of them and he and Rika left the balcony.

'Bloody Germans,' moaned Jane, *sotto voce.* 'The tennis is fine but afterwards. . . . Everything is so God-damned serious. We haven't heard either of them laugh all week, have we James? And the tennis clothes. Do you know Rika has a different outfit for every day they're here? Every bloody day! Can you believe it?'

'And what about Hans' rackets?' James said. 'It's not as if he is a great player but he's got five rackets here. Five! Every one is the best part of two hundred quid and he's had one restrung already as he thought it might have lost a bit of tension.'

James pointed to his Maxply. 'That racket is four years old and I've never had it restrung. It's good enough for me. *Senor.*' He beckoned to a waiter. 'One gin tonic, one beer and for you, Liz?' Liz refused. She had hardly started her first one. 'That's the other thing with Hans and Rika – they don't even drink – well, not proper drinks, just fizzy water so Jane and I finish up half cut 'cos we're so bloody bored. We really must try and find another couple, Jane, if we can. I don't think I can take another week of them.'

The waiter brought over the drinks and put yet another bar chit on the table.

'Got to make room for that one,' James said and left the table.

Jane leant towards Liz. 'I wanted a word with you on your own, Liz. Has Tom mentioned this idea the boys have got for the weekend?'

'No, what idea?'

'Oh well, he certainly will. For God's sake don't let on I've told you but apparently there is this golf course near Valencia – El Sal something – anyway its reckoned to be the best in Europe and the boys want to drive up there on Saturday, stay the night, play all day Sunday and either come back late that night or maybe not till Monday. Gilbert told me at lunchtime but maybe Tom is waiting for the right moment. Anyway we girls are obviously invited but I can't say I'm that keen. In fact not to put too fine a point on it I'd probably be bored stiff. The thing is I don't think I could very well be the odd one out but if you would like to stay down here as well, that would be fine.'

Liz's mind was racing. The idea of thirty-six hours or possibly even forty-eight with Tony, and a perfect alibi, just sounded too good to be true. But what about Margaret and Sue? Would they go or stay? Jane was the one she knew and liked best. But dare she tell her about Tony? She must find out a bit more first.

'Do you know what Margaret and Sue are doing?'

'I haven't spoken to them myself but Gilbert seemed to think they would be pretty keen on a weekend at a posh hotel. Apparently there is a Parador right on the golf course.'

'Really. And what about you? Do you have any plans for the weekend?'

'Well, I expect I'll play quite a bit of tennis.'

'And what about in the evenings?'

'We could go out couldn't we? Have dinner together and then perhaps go up to Yesterdays for an hour or two?

We might get picked up by two gorgeous men. Oh, Liz, say you'll stay here with me.'

'Jane, you're too keen. I don't think you're telling me the whole story.'

'No, Liz, you're right. OK but for God's sake don't tell a soul.'

'No, of course not. Go on.'

'The thing is James is here on his own. He's separated from his wife and he keeps saying how he would like to take me out to dinner and – well, whatever – there's nothing in it with James and me but it just, well, sounds fun to go out with someone else for a change and if you were here to give me an alibi, well then no one need know and no one gets hurt. What do you think?'

'Would you stay on the complex? Isn't that a bit dangerous?'

'Yes, I suppose it is but there's no choice is there? I mean Gilbert is bound to ring sometime and he is going to expect me to answer the phone. I can't be out all the time.'

'No, not unless you told Gilbert you wouldn't be there.' Liz's brain was still working overtime. This could all be perfect. It was just a question of working out the details. She would have to tell Jane about Tony. After all they were going to help each other.

'You see, Jane,' Liz said, 'I have had a very similar proposition but never imagined it was going to be possible to take it up.'

'No. Gosh. Really! Who is it? Is it Tony?'

'Well, yes it is actually but never mind about that for the moment. Let's think. I know. What if we say to Gilbert and Tom "You go off and enjoy yourselves but we want some fun as well!" Yes I've got it. We are always moaning that the boys will never take us to Murcia to shop at El Corte Ingles and have dinner at Rincon de Pepe. We could say we're going to do all that and spend the night in

51

Murcia. They're going to spend a night at an hotel. Why shouldn't we?'

'Crumbs, that's brilliant Liz! Do you do this sort of thing often?'

'No, not at all, it's the first time in fact but it certainly gets the brain cells working. You must come and have coffee tomorrow morning and we'll sort out the final details but in the meantime not a word to Gilbert and I won't say anything to Tom, assuming he mentions it, other than to signify a sort of grudging assent and a slight reluctance to go with them. Talking of Tom, I'd better get back to the flat. He's sure to be there by now.'

James was coming back to their table, having changed his shirt.

'I must go James. It was nice meeting you and thanks for the drink. See you tomorrow, Jane.'

'Yes, sure thing Liz. About 10 to 10.30 I should think.'

Liz could see them talking earnestly, their heads close together as she went down the stairs from the balcony. I hope the boys still want to go to Valencia this weekend she was thinking but above all I hope Tony is free on Saturday night and all day Sunday. What a let-down it would be if he were booked solid and couldn't or wouldn't cancel his arrangements. But he would – the afternoon had been good for him as well and his last words had been that she must try and fix something so that they could have longer together. No, everything was working out just fine. She felt on top of the world. Full of wellbeing, her mind clear, and with the sun going down behind Los Altos it was going to be another lovely day tomorrow. She swung round the corner to their flat and sure enough Tom was there sitting on the patio reading the *Telegraph* with a glass of wine on the table in front of him.

'There you are,' he said. 'Thought you'd left me.'

'No such luck I'm afraid. I've just been having a drink with Jane and her tennis crowd. How was the golf?'

'It was good enough rather than brilliant, I suppose. No one played particularly well but I seem to have sorted out the putting with my half hour on the putting green and didn't three putt once. What do you want to do this evening? Harold asked if we'd like to eat early and go round there for some bridge and Dick and Gilbert were talking about going down to the piano bar later on.'

'Well, unless you think it would be rude to Harold and Margaret I think I'd rather go to the piano bar. They take their bridge so seriously and play their cards so slowly. It's not as if they are any good and you know I can't handle their endless post mortems.'

Besides Tony might be at the piano bar she was thinking and she might get a chance to mention the weekend.

'Yes, that's fine. I told Harold you'd probably rather do some dancing, knowing your reaction to his bridge. I'll give him a ring.'

'Why not ask if they'd like to join us for supper? That sounds less rude and we've got loads of salad. Besides we were at their place last evening.'

'Good idea,' Tom said getting up and walking towards the phone. 'What time shall I say?'

'Oh, about eight I should think. We've got some cold ham and it won't take long to make the salad and we've got cheese and fruit.'

Tom dialled Harold's number.

'Hello, mate,' she heard Tom say. 'Look, Liz isn't too keen on bridge, more interested in tripping the light fantastic but why don't you come here and have a bite to eat at about eight? Great, see you then. Bye.' 'Better check we're OK for booze. Hm. Wine is all right but a bit low on gin and even worse on tonic. I'll just nip up to Bellaluz and sort that out. Is there anything you want?'

'No, I don't think so. Oh, wait a sec. Yes, if you want

salade Niçoise perhaps you could get some anchovies. A tin will do as I don't expect they will have any fresh ones.'

'OK, back in a few minutes. I'll do the salad for you if you like when I get back.'

He went out and she heard the car drive down the hill. She walked over to the phone and dialled 1216.

'Hello, Tony Seddon speaking.'

'Hi, it's me. It seems ages since I saw you.'

'Far too long. I haven't moved since you left. I don't want to lose the taste and smell of you. Is twelve o'clock tomorrow all right?'

'I haven't spoken to Tom yet but I'm sure it will be, but listen, I've got something much more exciting to say. You know you said a couple of hours wasn't long enough. How does sometime on Saturday through to Sunday night sound?'

'God, you don't half work fast. It sounds absolute heaven but are you sure about this as I will have to do a heck of a lot of rearranging?'

'I'm ninety per cent sure but I'll be at the piano bar later on. By then I should know for certain. Will you be there?'

'Sure as hell I will be now. Save the best dance for me sweetheart,' Tony said with a Humphrey Bogart accent. 'How on earth have you managed all this in not much more than an hour?'

'It's a long story, Tony and I'll tell you about it later but I think the gods must be on our side. I'm so excited. I must go now. Bye.'

She put the phone down and began to lay the table and get things out of the fridge for supper. She was glad Tom was going to do the salad. Her thoughts were so full of Tony and the weekend that she would probably make a complete hash of it and Tom always made a lovely dressing – every time it was slightly different because he never measured any quantities and sometimes the ingredients varied but it was always good. Tom came back with the gin, tonics and anchovies.

'Would you like a drink, luv?'

'No, I'm fine thanks. It's going to be a long evening and I had quite a big glass of wine with Jane.'

Tom started making the salad.

'Have you got any plans for the weekend?' he asked.

This was it Liz thought.

'No, I don't think so. There's no real difference on holiday is there? It's not as if we are Catholics and go to mass.'

'No, I suppose not. The thing is we were talking to a chap at lunchtime and he was raving about this course called El Saler – I think you've heard me mention it too – anyway it's just this side of Valencia and is rated the best course in Europe. A bit like an English links in part but with more trees and with a Parador right in the middle of it. So what we were thinking was, that we could drive up on Saturday morning, play in the afternoon, stay the night at the Parador, play 18 or even 36 holes on Sunday and then, if we felt up to it drive back that night, or, if we felt totally shattered, stay the Sunday night as well and drive back on Monday morning. It just seems silly flying over the course year after year and never playing it when it is only a little over three hours drive away. What do you think?'

Liz paused. She must not appear too eager.

'Who exactly is we?' she asked.

'Well obviously Harold, Dick, Gilbert and me and any of you girls who would like to come.'

Liz was thinking. Obviously she and Jane weren't going if they could possibly help it but if Sue and Margaret went that would be marvellous. It would be very dangerous if Sue and Margaret knew what was going on and fatal if they wanted to come to Murcia, unless they had got chaps in tow as well and she didn't think that was likely. No. Murcia must seem like a last minute idea.

'Hm, I don't know that I'm all that keen. It's quite a long drive isn't it, especially in a Seat, and you know I don't like hotels much.'

This was one of the reasons they had bought at La Manga as Liz never really enjoyed staying at hotels and liked having lots of her own things around her, eating and drinking when they wanted and what they wanted. Although she did not consider herself a fussy eater it seemed very rare that there was anything on an hotel menu that really appealed to her.

'I'll talk to the others,' she said, 'but I don't imagine any of us are going to throw a complete wobbly if you leave us for a day or two. It's not as if we're not used to being golf widows is it? No, that's fine. You men all go and I'll have a talk with the others. It could be, for example, that Sue and Margaret will go with you and Jane and I will live it up here. We'll sort something out. Don't you worry.'

Soon afterwards Harold and Margaret came round and after a couple of drinks they sat down to supper.

'Has Tom mentioned this Valencia trip?' Margaret asked excitedly. 'It sounds marvellous don't you think? I've always wanted to go to Valencia and there is this Parador right in the middle of the golf course just a few minutes walk from the beach. I think the Parador is a modern one but even so. We've never spent a night away from here all the time we've been coming down and I think it sounds great.'

'Yes, funnily enough we were talking about it just before you came. I can certainly understand the chaps wanting to go but I don't know that I'm all that keen. Still I'll see what Jane and Sue think. I certainly wouldn't want to be the odd one out would I?'

'Actually if two of you come that would probably be ideal,' Harold said, 'and it is pretty obvious Margaret is one of them. We'll need two cars anyway with all the golf clubs but if all eight of us go that would mean three cars which is quite a convoy. That was delicious Liz, and you, of course Tom, you obviously have a second career available as a *chef du salade*.'

Tom laughed. 'I don't think so somehow. I enjoy it occasionally but if I had to do it I think I'd hate it. The mental stimulus of negotiation is much more in my line – giving just enough to satisfy the other guy but keeping a little more back so that you know you've won the day in the end.'

5

Soon afterwards they walked down to the piano bar where the pianist was already in full swing with the *afficionados* grouped on stools around him, their drinks standing on the highly polished surface of the grand piano. Dick and Gilbert had not yet arrived so the four of them spread themselves round two adjacent tables to leave room for them. Harold ordered drinks from a passing waiter. Liz saw that Tony was already there sharing a table with a couple she had seen him with before but to date he had made no show of recognition, although she was sure he knew she was there. There was a sort of electricity between them that had immediately drawn her eyes towards his table as soon as she had entered the room.

Just then Gilbert, Jane, Dick and Sue came and joined them and after ordering more drinks, Gilbert asked Liz to dance.

'What are you going to do at the weekend then?' Gilbert asked almost before they had reached the tiny dance floor.

'I don't know yet. I want to talk with Jane and Sue. All I know at the moment is that Margaret is very keen to go and I'm not wildly struck on the idea.'

'Well, I can help you there because the four of us have been talking about it. Sue is quite keen on going but Jane seems so besotted with her wretched tennis that she won't even consider it. I'm quite hurt, actually. Why couldn't she give up a couple of days' tennis?'

'Come off it, Gilbert,' Liz cried. 'What's sauce for the gander and all that. When do you give up a couple of days' golf?'

'Touché. Anyway if you stay here I'll feel ever so much happier. Keep an eye on her, Liz, see she doesn't go off the rails.' Liz looked at him quizzically.

'You're not really worried are you Gilbert?'

'N-No, well perhaps just a bit. It's just she wouldn't even consider coming to Valencia with us and she seems a bit thick with some chap at the tennis club – plays all her tennis with him and I think she's drinking rather a lot. She's usually very flushed when she gets back from the club.'

'Probably just lots of running about in this hot weather I should think. I'll keep an eye on her for you, Gilbert. Don't you worry. You go off and enjoy your golf and make sure you take the money off Tom. I think he's winning too often.'

'You can say that again. Thanks Liz, I feel much better already and thanks for the dance.'

They walked back to their table and Liz saw that Tony was now in their party. That was clever to come over when she was on the dance floor she thought, very subtle.

'Tony says your first lesson was very encouraging, luv,' Tom said. 'He thinks if he gives you another three or four you'll have the rudiments of a swing and then it's up to me to give you the opportunity to play in England and lots of encouragement.'

'Great,' Liz said. 'When's my next lesson?'

'How about twelve tomorrow?' said Tony as if he had never mentioned it before.

'Absolutely fine, I'll look forward to it.'

The men now started talking about El Saler and their

forthcoming trip. Tony, of course, had played there and had seen Bernard Langer shoot his incredible 62 which many people thought was probably the finest round of golf that had ever been played.

'Liz, why don't you want to come with us?' asked Sue.

'I think "don't want to come" is probably a bit strong but I don't like hotels, never have, and as you and Margaret want to go I am perfectly happy to stay here with Jane. We'll be fine here, won't we Jane?'

'Sure thing, Liz,' replied Jane. 'So that's settled, is it? Sue and Margaret will see the boys behave themselves and Liz and I will ensure nothing happens to La Manga in your absence and that there is a warm welcome for you when you get back.'

The pianist was playing *Lady in Red*, one of Liz's favourite songs and she hoped someone would ask her to dance – well not someone – she hoped Tony would ask her to dance.

As if reading her thoughts he said, 'Would you like to dance, Liz? It's a fair trade – you teach me to dance and I'll teach you to play golf.'

'I'd love to. Thank you.'

Together they walked over to the dance floor by the piano. Tony put his arm round her and they moved rhythmically to the music. Was there nothing this man was not good at Liz wondered. There was certainly nothing she could teach him about dancing.

'You seem to have got everything worked out on your side don't you?' he said. 'I've had a look through my diary for the weekend and I could be free from lunchtime on Saturday until first thing Monday morning. How does that sound?'

'Absolute heaven,' Liz replied, 'though from the sound of it I don't think we can count on having Sunday night together. Do you think we could go away somewhere on

Saturday night as I don't think I could really relax here. I mean a lot of people know me and the whole world seems to know you. I think we would be asking for trouble.'

'Yes, I think that is a great idea. Have you anywhere in mind?'

'I have actually. In Murcia there is supposed to be a marvellous restaurant called Rincon de Pepe and it's got its own hotel attached. I've been wanting to go there for ages and perhaps do a bit of shopping at El Corte Ingles but it has never seemed possible before because Tom is too tired in the evening or has got a very early start next morning.'

'That sounds absolutely perfect,' Tony replied. 'I've never been to Rincon de Pepe either but have always wanted to. But isn't there a problem with Jane? From what I heard you are keeping each other company aren't you?'

'Ah! I haven't come to that bit yet. The wonderful part is that Jane has got something going this weekend as well so to some extent we will join up with them, but neither Tom nor Gilbert will think it strange if we – that is Jane and me – not you and me go off to Murcia together so we can give each other perfect alibis.'

'Yes, that really is clever. You're not going to share a bedroom with Jane, are you?'

'No chance if the alternative is sharing one with you. Jane is coming round for a coffee tomorrow morning when we will sort out the final details, but that is the gist of it and if there are any slight changes I can let you know at twelve. OK?'

'Absolutely. Had I better take you back to your table? I don't want to but . . . and can I just say that the excellence of your dancing is only exceeded by your fellatio.'

Liz felt herself blush but didn't think it would show with the dim lighting in the piano bar.

'I just hope you're not disappointed with anything else.'

They went back to the table and soon afterwards Tony left them and joined some of his other friends. Tom and Liz stayed until about twelve-thirty and then walked up to their flat together, Tom holding Liz's hand as they walked up the steps. We must look a happily married couple, Liz mused, and we are – my feelings for Tony don't affect my feelings for Tom or make me unhappy being his wife. The strength and solidity of her relationship with Tom just lacked the excitement of what was happening between her and Tony, and why shouldn't she have a little excitement, or even a lot of excitement she thought remembering the hour or so in Tony's bedroom that afternoon.

'Have you got any plans for the weekend?' Tom asked.

'Not at the moment but Jane is coming round for a coffee tomorrow and I'm sure we'll sort something out. I'd quite like to go to Murcia if I can persuade Jane to miss a day's tennis.'

'That sounds a nice idea and I'm sure Gilbert would be relieved. I think he is quite worried about Jane and some chap she's met at the tennis club and seems to be spending a lot of time with.' They had reached the flat and it was not long before they were in bed. Liz cuddled up against Tom's back but in her mind she saw Tony and imagined cuddling up against him, but somehow she didn't picture herself cuddling his back.

Jane arrived next morning punctually at ten just after Liz had finished her morning's chores. Liz put on the coffee machine.

'Everything is working out pretty well, don't you think?' Jane said.

'Marvellous, I just can't believe how well. Have you spoken to James yet? What does he think about going to Murcia?'

'He thinks it's a great idea too but he wants us to play our usual tennis in the afternoon and then go on to Murcia afterwards to arrive sort of seven to seven thirty in the evening. That would be all right wouldn't it? What are you and Tony going to do anyway? I must say he is a bit of a dish. You must have discussed it with him on the dance floor last night. I saw you talking nineteen to the dozen and I very much doubt if it was all about your golf swing.'

'We have not finalised the details but he is very keen on Rincon de Pepe and I know he is free after lunch so I might try and persuade him to come up rather earlier than you and James. I'm glad you think he is a dish too. I think he is fantastic. I never thought I'd be found attractive by a man like him at my age but isn't it great for one's ego?'

'Certainly is. I suppose James is not that good looking but he must be at least ten years younger than me. Anyway, back to business, had we better check that the accommodation is available?'

'Yes, good idea. I'll ring Rincon de Pepe now and book two rooms. Now let me see, one had better be in my name, or yours and then we'll want a table or tables for dinner. What do you think? Shall we eat together?'

'Oh, yes, I think so. Give us a chance to compare notes,' Jane giggled, 'and I think book one room in your name and the other in James'. Hislop is his surname. Do you know the phone number?'

'No, but I can soon find out.' Liz picked up the telephone and dialled nine for the operator.

'*Hola*, can you tell me the number of Rincon de Pepe in Murcia, *por favor*?' There was a pause. '212249, *gracias*.'

Liz replaced the receiver, picked it up and redialled.

There was another pause while Liz waited for her call to be answered. 'Rincon de Pepe? *Habla ingles?* Oh, good. I would like to book two double rooms for Saturday night. Yes, this Saturday. One is in the name of Waldren,

W-A-L-D-R-E-N of La Manga Club and the other in the name of Hislop, H-I-S-L-O-P also of La Manga Club and can I reserve a table for four in your restaurant that evening?' Liz put her hand over the mouthpiece.

'What time do we want the table, Jane?'

'Oh, not too late – but thinking about it not too early either.' Again Jane giggled.

'You never know what might come up. How about nine thirty?'

'Sounds good to me,' Liz said and she took her hand away from the mouthpiece.

'*A las nueve y media, por favor. Bueno, muchas gracias. Adios.*'

'So far so good,' Liz said.

So far so very good,' Jane replied. 'If you and Tony are going to get there in the afternoon I presume you will look in at El Corte Ingles so can you buy something for me? Anything really so long as it's in one of their posh green bags. I'll settle up with you when I see you.'

'Yes, of course I can do that. I think I must go there. Tom would never believe I had been to Murcia if I didn't buy something – I've got a reputation to live up to. Now, what else is there to think about?'

'What about if Gilbert rings? He'll get put through to your room won't he and I won't be there. I hope he doesn't ring at an awkward time.'

'So do I, or Tom either for that matter. I don't think it should be a problem. I'll just say you're in the bath or something and that you'll ring back in a few minutes. Then I ring your room, you phone back and Bob's your uncle. *No problema.* Is there anything else?'

'Hmm. No. I don't think so. I must say I'm jolly impressed with the way you are organising all this. Are you sure you've never done this sort of thing before?'

'No, never. How about you?'

'If you mean have I ever been unfaithful the answer has

to be yes. A few times at home but never anything like this when I'm on holiday with Gilbert. It used to be so easy at home because Gilbert used to go to the States two or three times a year on business and he nearly always went during term time so when the children were away at boarding school it was all so easy. I did have bit of a problem once. It must have been about five years ago. I'd been away with this bloke for the weekend and he was driving me home at about ten o'clock on Sunday night and we were following this taxi up the road. I wasn't thinking about it at all until it turned in our drive and we all but followed him in. I suddenly realised it was Gilbert, back a day early. "Drive on," I said so it was round to the station, tender goodbye and my turn to grab a taxi. It was OK 'cos I said I'd spent the weekend with an old girl friend of mine in Dorset and all I had to explain was why I hadn't driven down, but if we had got back half an hour earlier – or Gilbert half an hour later – it could have all been a bit of the *flagrante delicto*. It's really very inconsiderate when husbands don't come back when they are supposed to. Apparently Gilbert had had a Monday meeting cancelled and thought he'd give me a nice surprise. Could have been some surprise.'

'What about Gilbert?' Liz asked. 'Is he the ever-loving faithful husband?'

'I think so, certainly at home, but he might have had something going in the States at one time. I remember thinking there were one or two refinements in his technique but I'd been a naughty girl while he had been away so thought I might have done something I didn't usually do and produced a different reaction from him. I don't think it pays to look into these things too deeply. We're reasonably happy – why rock the boat I say? What about Tom?'

'Oh, I'm sure he's had the odd fling but like you I don't

think a searching cross-examination is going to achieve anything. I'm sure he's never had a serious relationship with anyone else and that is the main thing. I do think you've got to be careful though. Gilbert is definitely worried about James. He's mentioned it to both Tom and me.'

'Christ, really! The old bugger! He hasn't said a word to me. Thanks for the warning. Anyway, I must be off to tell James the plan but as far as our husbands are concerned, and everyone else for that matter apart from Tony and James, we're leaving here tomorrow after lunch aiming to shop at El Corte Ingles and then dinner, bed and breakfast at Rincon de Pepe. Right?'

'Right, and one of us had better take whichever of our cars the men don't take. In fact, rather than have all our well laid plans scuppered by an accident and an insurance hassle, if it's our car I'll drive and if it's yours you're driving. OK?'

'Yes, that's fine. See you in Murcia at about nine thirty tomorrow, if not before.'

6

Jane left the flat and walked down the hill towards the tennis club and Liz saw it was a quarter past eleven. Still three quarters of an hour to go before my lesson, she mused. Perhaps Tony would be impressed if she went down to the practice ground half an hour early and hit some balls. Yes, that's what she would do. She went down to the Pro's shop, bought a ticket for fifty balls and walked to the practice ground. She went up to the young Spanish boy who dispensed the buckets of balls and handed him her ticket. He passed her a small bucket of balls.

'Feefty balls, mees. You have clubs?'

Suddenly Liz realised that without Tony she had no clubs. What a fool she was. She looked round to see if Tony was on the practice ground, but he was nowhere to be seen.

'N-No,' she said. 'I thought my friend would be here.'

'Don't worry,' the Spanish boy said, 'I get you club.'

He ran off and was soon back with a rather battered four iron. 'Ees good club. I show you.' He took a ball out of the bucket, took an enormous, if rather unstylish swing and the ball flew away carrying the 150 metre mark.

'You want use my club – one hundred pesetas,' he said holding the club towards her.

'Yes, well, er, thank you, I will,' Liz said reaching in her purse for a one hundred peseta coin. The boy looked disappointed. 'You no teep? Ees good club.'

Liz remembered that except in shops or markets where one tended to haggle, if anything, everything else in Spain demanded a tip. She opened her purse again and produced a further 25 pesetas. The boy beamed.

'You can play 'ere,' he said.

Liz put her purse down beside the bucket of balls and started to play shots with the very short waist-high back swing Tony had taught her. She was quite pleased with the way things were going, especially with such an old club which had a very hard slippery grip. She had noticed that the clubs Tony lent her all had quite soft tacky grips and this obviously made it easier to hold the club firmly but not too tightly. Everything must be relaxed Tony had said. Knees slightly flexed. Elbows slightly bent. Head inclined forward. Shoulders relaxed. She looked round her at the other people on the practice ground. There were a couple of young men at the far end of the line who were obviously very good players who hit the balls what seemed like miles with a minimum of fuss and effort. But there was a middle-aged man near her who was concentrating like mad but making the game look so difficult. His legs were rigid, his arms held out like ram rods and he picked the club up almost vertically with very little shoulder turn, and not low accompanied by a pivot from the waist, as Tony taught. He then lunged at the ball which seemed to go in every direction except the one intended and a very short distance, often less than Liz's shots which were nearly all straight and a fairly consistent fifty or sixty yards. The man could feel Liz's eyes on him and he turned towards her.

'Bloody stupid game,' he said and flailed at another ball which shot off the toe of his club only just missing the person on his right. Just then the Spanish boy came up to Liz.

'You make more swing,' he said. 'Ball go more far.'

Liz decided to take his advice. She swung her club back above her shoulder and brought it down. It banged into the ground about six inches behind the ball which trickled slowly forwards for three or four yards. How ridiculous she thought. She tried again with a similar result. She tried a third time and the ball went low and a bit right but it travelled eighty or ninety yards. That's a bit better she said to herself.

'What on earth do you think you're doing?'

She turned quickly to see Tony only a few yards away.

'Oh, hello. I had a bit of time before my lesson so thought I'd come down and have a little practice. That's not wrong is it?'

'No, it's great if you practice what I taught you, but you're not ready for a full swing yet.'

Liz realised that Tony was now working. He was one of those people who could switch on and off like an electric light. If he was working that was all he thought of and if he thought at all about the previous afternoon in his hotel bedroom or the coming weekend which could and should be idyllic, it was very much in the background of his mind and now he was concentrating on developing her golf swing.

'Where the devil did you get that club from?' he said.

'The Spanish boy lent it to me. It cost me 100 pesetas plus teep.'

'Bloody robbery. Give it back to him and we'll carry on from where we left off yesterday.'

'What, here on the practice ground?' Liz said chuckling. Tony did not reply so she took the club back to the Spanish boy and followed Tony to a quiet section of the line of people hitting balls. He passed her a five iron.

'Now then, let's see how much you remember. First of all the grip.' Liz was determined to get some acknowledgement of yesterday. She clasped the club in both hands and held it close to her mouth making licking motions with her tongue as if she were holding an ice cream cone.

'I think it was something like that,' she said smiling at him.

'For Christ's sake Liz – don't remind me. I've found it hard to think about anything else since but can we concentrate on golf for an hour?'

'If we must,' Liz replied.

She was happy now. She had achieved her objective of an admission from him that yesterday had been special. She held the club properly now with an interlocking grip and the Vs between her thumbs and forefingers pointing towards her chin.

'Yes, that's pretty good – you could get your right hand slightly more round the club.' He adjusted the position to his satisfaction. 'And now the stance.'

She stood to a ball and positioned it about mid-way between her feet.

'And where are you aiming?'

'Towards the cricket pavilion, I think.'

Tony laid a club down touching the front of her feet. 'Can you see where that is pointing?'

Liz looked along the line of the club and saw that it was pointing well to the left of where she thought. She brought her left foot forward a few inches.

'Is that better?'

'Yes, that's fine.'

She then started hitting balls with a waist-high back swing initially but towards the end of the lesson it was about shoulder high and the balls were going fairly straight quite consistently and only a few did not get airborne. When it came to one o'clock Tony said, 'That's really good, but please don't try and run before you can walk. Just keep taking short swings remembering to pivot and keep your head still. Are you going to the 37th?'

'Yes, I'll go and wait for Tom.'

As they walked up to the club she was able to explain all she had arranged with Jane, the hotel and the restaurant. Tony was obviously looking forward to it as much as she was. She just hoped that Tom would take their car so that she and Tony could go in the Porsche. Although it did not worry her driving on the right-hand side of the road she still had to concentrate quite hard, especially in the hired Seat as opposed to the Peugeot 205 she drove at home. She just wanted to be able to curl up in the big passenger seat in the Porsche and relax.

When they arrived at the 37th Tom and his crowd were already there and they called for them to come over to their table. Tony asked Liz if she would like a drink but Tom insisted on giving the order and asked Tony what progress Liz was making.

'Very good really – like all beginners she wants to hit it too far too soon. When I got down to the practice ground this morning there she was trying a full swing with some dreadful club she had borrowed, or rather hired, from the Spanish boy who gives out the balls and it wasn't going too well, but I got her to settle down and relax and I'm very pleased with the progress she's made.'

'That's great,' Tom said. 'Obviously I'll have to see what I can do about getting her into a club at home, but it's a hell of a problem in our part of the country without a handicap. Thanks very much anyway, for what you are doing. I'm delighted Liz is showing an interest in playing at last.' He turned to Liz. 'And how did coffee go? Have you sorted out your weekend plans with Jane?'

'Oh, yes darling. Everything's fixed. We're going to Murcia, leaving here tomorrow after lunch. We'll have a good look round, including a little visit to El Corte

Ingles, I expect – that could be a bit expensive – and then we've got a room booked at Rincon de Pepe.' She turned to Gilbert, 'it's in my name if you want to ring Jane anytime. Hang on I'll give you the number.' She rummaged in her purse. 'Yes, here it is – 'it's 212249 from here but I expect you've got to put 968 in front of that from Valencia – and then we've got a table booked in the restaurant in the evening. I'm so looking forward to it,' she added breathlessly, and smiled – a smile meant for Tony but she could not aim it at him too directly.

'That sounds really good,' said Tom, 'except for our bank balances. What do you think, Gilbert?'

'I'm absolutely delighted that Jane is going away with Liz and unless they go mad shopping, which they might have done in Valencia anyway, I can't see why it should cost anymore than if they had come to the Parador with us.'

'No, you're probably right,' said Tom, 'and although I'm sure I'd enjoy a meal at this Rincon place, I'm frankly delighted to get out of an afternoon trekking round the shops in Murcia. What about you, Tony? Are you working all weekend while the rest of us lead the good life?'

'No, not all the time. I'm booked pretty solidly on Saturday, but some friends have asked me down to their place at Mazarron so I'm going down there on Saturday evening and will spend Sunday with them. I'm hoping to go out deep-sea fishing on their boat so that should be fun,' Tony lied.

'So, everyone's organised, that's great. Dick has booked three double rooms at the Parador and we've been told there should be no problem getting on the course so all we want is good weather and everyone should have a good time.'

Tony got up from his chair. 'I must grab a quick

sandwich – my next lesson is at two. Can I get anyone a drink before I go?'

'No, we're fine,' Harold replied. 'We'll probably see you on Monday unless we bump into each other this evening.'

Tony went off to the food counter and soon the rest of them left the bar and went off to their respective apartments. As Tom and Liz walked to their car Liz said, 'Are you taking this one tomorrow?'

'Well, I'd like to because you know I always prefer to drive, but what about you? Will you want it?'

'As long as Gilbert leaves his I certainly shan't need a car. In fact I'd really prefer to be driven, especially by Jane as she's a jolly good driver.'

'OK, that's fine. I'm sure Gilbert will be quite happy for me to drive so we shall probably travel together with all the golf clubs and luggage and the others can go in Harold or Dick's car.'

Liz could not believe how well everything was going. It was as if she and Tony were meant to have this time together. In an absolutely ideal world she would have preferred it to have been just the two of them but she liked Jane, and although she was not too impressed with James it wasn't as if they would see much of him. It was really just going to be dinner as she was sure she and Tony would have their *desayuno* in the room next morning. Spanish breakfasts were not much different to French breakfasts except that they always included a sweet cake, which neither she nor Tom had ever been able to face on the rare occasions they had stayed in a Spanish hotel.

With everything now organised Liz couldn't wait for tomorrow lunch time, but this was almost twenty-four hours away. How was she going to fill all this time? She didn't really want to spend it all with Tom either but what was the alternative?

'What are your plans this afternoon?' she said as they arrived at the flat.

'Dunno really,' Tom said. 'Sit in the sun, do the crossword, read a bit, pleasure you perhaps. What do you think?'

The idea of Tom making love to her suddenly felt abhorrent yet in all their married life she could hardly think of a time when she had actually refused Tom.

'It's certainly a lovely afternoon to sit on the patio and read but my hair is a mess and I'd like to have it done before we go to Murcia. I'm sure all the women in Murcia will be very smart, especially at Rincon de Pepe. If you don't mind I think I'll go down to Los Belones at four thirty and see if I can get a shampoo and set. The *peluqueria* is always so busy on Saturday morning and I shall never understand why Spanish hairdressers don't have an appointment system.'

'OK, that's fine. If you're going to do that I think I'll play nine holes round the North course at the same time. I'd quite like to practise my long irons ready for El Saler.'

They had their lunch time snack, and polished off the crossword – Liz was pleased there were no embarrassing clues today – and at about four fifteen she dropped Tom off at the Clubhouse.

'Shall I pick you up on my way back?' she asked.

'Yes, that would be great. Don't bother to wait if I'm not there but I'll probably be in by the time you're back and I won't find it too much of a hardship having a beer while I wait.'

Liz was tempted to pop down to Room 216 just in case Tony was there but she resisted temptation. Not too long to wait now and they must not take unnecessary risks and spoil it all. She drove down to Los Belones and almost automatically bought some milk, bread, cold ham, eggs and fruit and then walked on to the *peluqueria*. Fortunately she did not have to wait very long as there was only one man in front of her who was having a trim. The young Spanish hairdresser did not speak an appreciable amount of English but with a bit of sign language and the help of another customer, who had just come in, Liz was able to make him understand how she wanted it set and was pleased with the result. He had flair and with his dark eyes and flashing smile she thought he would make a fortune in Oxted from the well-to-do housewives in the area. He charged 750 pesetas and she gave him 1,000. It was overtipping but she paid about ten pounds for the same thing at home so at little more than a fiver it still seemed very cheap. He thanked her effusively.

'*Proxima semana, cortar?*' he said making snipping motions in the air. Liz was not quite sure what he meant but it obviously included cutting her hair. She would have been quite happy to have him cut it but she was going back to England on Tuesday and did not know how to explain this to him.

'*Quizas,*' she said. Perhaps was one of the few words she knew but she felt so inadequate in this sort of situation knowing so little Spanish. She would really like to have Spanish lessons and a thought suddenly struck her. Tony came to La Manga much more than she and Tom but there was no real reason why she should not come down on her own. She must be able to organise a week or two on her own some time when Tony was down. She could have Spanish lessons during the day at the School on the Strip when Tony was giving his golf lessons but in the evenings . . . and the nights. . . . The idea really excited her. She must start working on it right away. She'd raise the subject with Tom first and if she could get a sort of grudging assent (she knew it would not be effusive if it meant Tom looking after himself) she could get some possible dates from Tony. She was sure he would be enthusiastic. What heaven it would be! Their apartment was used so little and when it was shut up for long periods it always got rather a musty smell and she spent hours the first few days going over all the tiled floors and walls with bleach and disinfectant and cleaning out all the cupboards. It was really good property maintenance to use it more. That would appeal to Tom as a surveyor, and she could give all the upholstery a good clean. She never got round to it when they were only there for a couple of weeks but on her own it would be different. The upholstery always got so badly stained when people carelessly sat down with sun oil still on their bodies and she thought her son, Peter, was probably the worst culprit of all. She couldn't think why she had not thought of this before, but then she had never had such an incentive before. A week or two's charring was hardly a turn-on, but a week or two with Tony with a bit of charring and a few Spanish lessons thrown in sounded really special.

She pulled in at the golf club and walked down to the 37th bar. There was no sign of Tom but Tony was there with one of his inevitable middle-aged couples. He got up from his chair.

'Would you like to join us?' he said. Liz sat down.

'Drink?'

'A small beer would be lovely,' Liz replied. 'Have you seen Tom? I've just been down to Los Belones and I said I'd look in on the way back.'

'No, I haven't seen him I'm afraid but I don't expect he'll be long. Your hair looks really nice. I'm sure anyone with you this weekend will feel really proud.' He smiled enigmatically. 'Sorry, I haven't introduced you. Liz Waldren, this is Fred and Marcia, two very old friends of mine. They live in Devon now but used to be Sheringham members and once a week for the last four years we have met up down here and I try and polish off a few of the rough edges that have developed in their game.'

'He's absolutely wonderful,' Marcia said. 'I've never found another golf professional who helps me so much. Every year when we go back to England we do well in the first few competitions we enter but it always wears off.'

Tony smiled, relishing the praise.

'You know the answer. Instead of coming to see me once a year you should come every few months.'

'Yes, but Sheringham is such a long way from Tavistock,' Fred said.

'Not nearly so far as La Manga, surely.'

'Ah, but this is not just a golf lesson, this is a holiday as well. We always enjoy our week or two out here and I can't get excited about going to Norfolk from Devon for a holiday.'

Just then Tom came in.

'There you are,' he said. 'See you got your hair done then.'

Liz introduced him to Fred and Marcia. It was so typical of Tom, Liz thought, that he never complimented her on her appearance. He noticed that she had had it done but he wouldn't say, 'That looks nice' or 'That style really suits you.' She always had to ask if he liked her clothes or her perfume and sometimes she wondered why she bothered but Tony had liked it, or said he did, and she had gone to the hairdresser's for him after all.

'Anyone like another drink?' Tom said. 'I'm dying for a pint.' Fred and Tony had another small beer to keep him company but Marcia and Liz refused.

'This is our last night,' Marcia said, 'and we're taking Tony out for a meal because he never charges us a proper commercial rate. Would you and your husband like to join us? We've heard of a restaurant at La Union which is supposed to be very good and we thought we'd like to try it. It's supposed to be genuinely Spanish and nearly all the clientele are Spanish.'

'It sounds a lovely idea to me,' Liz said, 'but we are here with six other friends and I don't know if Tom has fixed up anything with them.'

At that moment Tom came back with the three beers.

'Darling, Marcia has asked if we'd like to join Fred, Tony and her for dinner this evening at a restaurant at La Union. It sounds a lovely idea to me but have you made any arrangements with the others?'

'No, I haven't actually. I'll be seeing plenty of them this weekend anyway. Sounds great. Where and when shall we meet?'

'Well, the three of us are all staying at the hotel so why don't we meet here about eightish, have a drink and go on to the restaurant when we are ready?' Fred said.

'Super,' Tom replied. 'We don't have to dress up for this place, do we? I hate wearing a tie in Spain.'

'Oh, I'm sure not, an open neck shirt and slacks seems to be acceptable just about everywhere. I can't believe El Vinagrero is any different.'

Liz turned to Marcia. 'Tell me. What's Fred's and your Spanish like? Ours is awful and I felt so inadequate in the hairdressers. I hadn't a clue how to express how I wanted my hair set and but for a fairly bilingual customer, I don't know how we'd have got on. I would really like to have some Spanish lessons down here, but I can't get any enthusiasm from Tom.'

'No, I am afraid we are just as bad. In fact it is one of the reasons we come here as one can get by without any Spanish. Still we're all right tonight, going out with Tony. He's marvellous and always seems to get on so well with the Spanish waiters, he has them eating out of his hand.'

And it's not just Spanish waiters, Liz thought.

'My Spanish is not really that good,' said Tony, 'I mean

I've never had any lessons so the grammar is very bad and I use lots of wrong tenses but I've been coming here for four or five weeks for the last five years and when I was on the tour I played in quite a few of the Spanish tournaments so I've picked up a lot of the Spanish colloquialisms and the Spaniards like that. They're really a very friendly and informal race and if you say something like *Como esta* which is the formal way of saying 'How are you' they will not react nearly as well as if you say '*Que tal*' which means the same thing. I've also got some Spanish tapes which I play in the car quite a bit, especially on the drive down here. I virtually know them by heart now, but they remind me of the sounds.'

'We should do that, Tom,' Liz said. 'You can get me a Spanish language course for my birthday. Isn't that an easy present?'

They finished their drinks and made their separate ways.

'You don't mind going out with them for dinner, do you?' Liz asked.

'No, not at all. They seem a pleasant couple and you know I always like meeting new people. I suppose I'm still slightly wary of Tony, but its probably only what Harold said and he's certainly good company. No, I'm looking forward to it and you're obviously keen to go.'

'Well, from what they say it is a real Spanish restaurant so, yes, I am looking forward to that as most of the places we go seem to have more English clients than Spanish and it's almost like going to a Spanish restaurant in London. I really am serious about having Spanish lessons. In fact I was wondering what you'd think of the idea if I came out on my own sometime for a week or two and I could go to lots of Spanish classes and give the flat a really good spring clean. You know how nasty it smells when we come out each time, and I don't

79

think the maids give it much more than a lick and a promise.'

'Doesn't sound much of a holiday,' Tom replied, 'but I don't see why not if that is what you really want to do. Perhaps you could go when I'm playing golf in the Hewitt or the Mellin or something.'

'I'm not thinking of it as a holiday, but I'm sure I could come sometime when you are away. I'll check your diary when we get back and try and find a suitable week or two. I think two weeks would be better if I'm to make any progress with the Spanish.'

When they arrived at the flat Tom helped her carry in the shopping and put it away. He stood behind her as she was reaching up to one of the cupboards, cupped her breasts in his hands and nuzzled her right ear.

'Fancy a quickie, old thing?'

Liz looked at her watch. 'Oh Tom, I think it would have to be too much of a quickie and besides I've only just had my hair done. I don't really want it mussed up just before we go out. Do you mind?' She smiled at him.

'Don't see that it makes much difference if I do or don't,' Tom said bitterly. 'Sex is only fun with an enthusiastic partner.'

He walked over to the shelf where they kept the drinks and poured a very large Scotch.

'D'you want anything or might it spoil your hair-do?' he said sarcastically.

'Oh, Tom, don't be like that. Come on then.'

Liz walked half way up the steps to the bedroom and held out a hand towards Tom.

'No thanks. I'll drink my Scotch on the patio and finish the paper.' Tom walked outside and Liz slowly took off her clothes and went through to the bathroom for her shower. She must not be like this, she thought. Tom was bound to get suspicious. She must give him a really good love when they got back from the restaurant, or perhaps in the morning before he left for El Saler. She couldn't have him going off feeling frustrated or, even worse, wondering what she was up to. She heard Tom come in from the patio and pour himself another drink. Oh, God, she thought, I do hope this isn't going to be one of those awful evenings when he gets drunk and is rude to everyone. It didn't happen often but when it did he became such a bore, and she wanted it to be a pleasant evening. She came downstairs with her towel wrapped round her like a sarong and put her arms round him.

'Darling, don't you think you've had enough? We'll be having another drink or two in a minute and there's bound to be lots of wine with dinner.'

'Don't know if I'll bother to go at all. I'm just the bloody gooseberry. If I don't go you can have a lovely dinner with your fancy man and the other two.'

'Oh darling, don't be silly. I love you. Tony didn't ask me out. Marcia invited us to join them. Don't be an old grumps. Come on, sit down in the chair and I'll give you a massage.'

Liz led him to the chair, took the drink from him, pulled off his shirt and went up to the bathroom to get some baby oil. She gently massaged his shoulders and neck. She could feel his tension lessening and she let his head fall back against her breasts. She leant forwards and kissed him tenderly on the lips. 'Now then, how about your shower?'

'Thanks,' Tom said gruffly. 'Sorry, I was being stupid.'

He went upstairs and Liz poured his drink down the sink. Hopefully he would think he had finished it when he came back downstairs.

I've never given him the slightest cause to be jealous before, she thought. She must be careful. Perhaps she shouldn't have joined Tony, Fred and Marcia at the bar, but it would have seemed rude if she hadn't. She must be especially nice to Tom that evening. It really would be too terrible if Tom suddenly decided he wouldn't go to El Saler after all. It just didn't bear thinking about if all her plans came to naught.

They got down to the bar just after eight and the others had not arrived. Liz had a glass of white wine and was pleased to see that Tom just had a small beer. His capacity for beer seemed almost infinite – Scotch was the danger with Tom.

The others arrived and soon they set off to La Union. Liz was pleased that Marcia asked for a ride in the Porsche so she sat in the front of the Seat while Tom drove her and Fred.

La Union was a small town about five miles away which used to cater for the mining industry, but now that the mines had closed down it was being developed with modern factories and also housed some of the workers from the big Repsol oil refinery down the road. It was in no sense a holiday resort and Liz was pleased to be going there to eat as she had only previously been there for the weekly market on Tuesdays when she was always fascinated by the noisy crowds of Spaniards gathered around the various stalls arguing and gesticulating but also buying, often in vast quantities. Liz liked the fruit and vegetable stalls in particular, the peppers, aubergines, cauliflowers and broccoli glistening fresh and about a quarter of the price they would be in England for vegetables of inferior quality and freshness. The fruit was also a joy to buy, oranges in particular being less than tenpence a pound, making it cheaper to have freshly squeezed orange juice than to buy it in packets.

They were following Tony's Porsche as he and Marcia had said they knew where the restaurant was and Tony was driving slowly to allow the Seat to keep up. They turned down the main street in La Union and then Tony turned right down a very narrow road which was only just wider than the Porsche. Tom chuckled and Liz could see why. They had obviously taken the wrong turning and now Tony had to turn left down a one-way street. This was not going to pose any particular problem in the little Seat but with very narrow roads, high curbs, low spoilers and cills it was quite a problem for Tony and Tom was enjoying every moment of his discomfiture.

'He doesn't get everything right then,' Tom said.

'It's rather a relief really,' Liz said lightly.

'Don't count on it,' Fred said from the back. 'I don't think Tony has ever been to this restaurant so Marcia was probably navigating.'

By now they had gone another couple of hundred yards and there was the restaurant on their right with adjoining bar. They could not park outside as the road was too narrow but just a little further on was a private car park reserved for patrons of El Vinagrero. They parked their cars and as they got out Tom called out. 'Bit of a problem, old son? You should get yourself a Seat. I made the corner in one.'

Tony said nothing but smiled.

'Wasn't that awful?' Marcia said, 'And it was all my fault. I told Tony to turn too soon. I thought we were there for the evening, or even worse that Tony was going to damage his lovely car.'

They decided to go straight to the restaurant, which had an obvious air of quality with white linen table cloths and napkins, lovely fresh fish on display in a cold counter and already about twenty well-to-do Spaniards were sitting at tables and the aroma of garlic, peppers and fish assailed their nostrils and made them realise how hungry they were. There was noise of life and laughter and Liz thought how much quieter an English restaurant would be with a comparable number of customers. A tall good looking young waiter in impeccable dinner jacket greeted them and showed them to a table in the far corner. Marcia took charge of the seating arrangements and put Tony at the head of the table with Liz on his left, next to Fred, while she sat on Tony's right next to Tom. How perfect Liz thought and she hadn't organised it so Tom could not complain.

They ordered a bottle of dry white wine as an aperitif while they looked at the menu which was entirely in Spanish. Tony was able to tell them what most of the dishes were but obtained the assistance of the waiter for a few of the more esoteric items. Liz was delighted that they all chose different things as she liked to see the various dishes. She ordered small red peppers stuffed with prawns which were served hot, Marcia had shell fish soup, Fred chose smoked salmon, Tom decided on a salad with palm hearts and prawns and Tony went for a warm salad with avocado and setas, the special mushrooms which are almost unobtainable in England but always seem readily available in good quality restaurants in France and Spain. To follow they ordered bass, sole, fillet steak, escallop and crab. Liz was interested to see what vegetables would be served with the main dishes, as, unless specially ordered, many restaurants served either no vegetables at all or sometimes just chips. Here the meat dishes came with chips but also delicious small green peppers, fried in oil, while the hot fish courses were served with chips and green beans.

They all thoroughly enjoyed their meal, offering tastes to each other as if they were old friends and the almost constant pressure of Tony's left leg against hers heightened Liz's enjoyment, although watching Marcia's face she wondered at one time what he was doing with his right leg. Whatever it was, Marcia was not complaining.

Tom shared the bill with Fred as Tony had not charged for the two lessons he had given Liz and when they got back to the club Fred, Marcia and Tony decided to have a night cap. Tom and Liz went straight back to their apartment, making the excuse that Tom had an early start in the morning and had still not done any packing for his weekend at El Saler.

'Wasn't that a super evening?' Liz said. 'Do you want to pack now or what?'

'Oh, "what", I think. You know I never pack the night before.' They hastily undressed and cleaned their teeth.

'Shall I hop on top of Pop?' Liz said. This was one of their favourite positions for making love and the expression had been adopted from one of their children's books about twenty years ago. With a minimum of foreplay Liz straddled Tom and began a rhythmic movement with her hips, alternatively leaning forwards so Tom could kiss her breasts and then leaning back pressing Tom's penis hard against her clitoris while Tom caressed her nipples with his thumbs.

'I'll miss this tomorrow,' he murmured, nuzzling her ear as Liz leant forward brushing his chest with her erect nipples.

'You better had,' Liz said as she felt Tom's penis begin to throb and they climaxed together before she collapsed on top of him, their sweat mingling on their chests and stomachs.

7

Tom was up at seven thirty next morning and went for a shower before grabbing a suitcase from the closet and packing the things he'd need for El Saler. Liz just put on her housecoat while she prepared breakfast. She would give the flat a good clean after Tom had gone and she wanted to press her cocktail dress so she would look immaculate for dinner at Rincon de Pepe.

'I'm sorry I was in a bad mood yesterday evening,' Tom said before he left. 'Buy yourself something nice in Murcia,' and he handed her forty thousand pesetas. 'I should pay the hotel with your Barclaycard or if Jane pays give her an English cheque for your half.' This could be a bit of a problem Liz thought, especially if Gilbert had said the same thing to Jane, and he probably had. They couldn't both pay for a double room, but of course she had booked one of them in her name. Oh, they would work something out.

'Oh, thank you Tom – that's very generous. Do you want me to look out for anything for you?'

'No, I don't think so, unless you see some bargain boxer shorts, I always seem to need them. Something with Spanish flamenco dancers perhaps.'

Liz laughed. 'I very much doubt if the Spanish go in for those sort of pants. Anyway have a lovely time at El Saler and play well. You've got the number of our hotel, haven't you?'

'Yep, I've got it somewhere. I expect I'll ring late this evening or early tomorrow. Take care.'

Tom kissed her lightly on the lips and left the flat carrying his clubs and suitcase.

After he had gone and she had waved to him as he drove past the flat, she thought again about the bills at the hotel because something like that could be crucial, and there was also dinner to think about. What they must do is ask for the bill for dinner to be split between the two rooms and then if she paid for Tony's and her room by card and Jane gave her a cheque for half that should be OK. It meant Tony was going to get a free weekend but she was sure he was worth it and half a dinner was not nearly enough to pay for her golf lessons. She just hoped that he wasn't one of these macho types about men paying bills. She would mention it in the car so there was no misunderstanding.

The morning seemed endless. By ten thirty the flat was spotless and by eleven she had ironed her dress. She didn't want to pack until the last minute to minimise creasing. Still two hours to go. She went out on to the patio with her book. She read the same page about six times but still had not taken in one word. She knew she wanted to go away with Tony for this weekend – wanted it more than anything, but what if she fell in love with him? What then? She didn't want to have her shower until just before one o'clock so that she was fresh when Tony arrived. She would go for a walk she decided. She put on a tee shirt, shorts and sneakers and walked down to the tennis club. She couldn't see anyone she knew so she ordered a coffee and sat on the verandah. She looked at her watch. Still only half past eleven. Still an hour and a half to go. She walked the long way back past Los Altos and then past the villas which backed on to the South course before climbing the steep hill to the flat. Now she was hot and sticky. She poured a cold *agua con gas* and drank it slowly before going through to the bedroom. She packed her case and then had a long cool shower, powdered her parts, applied deodorant and a touch of perfume. Not too much so early in the day. She was still worried about Tony picking her up. What if she were seen getting into Tony's car with a case? Some of the residents only lived a few doors away and Tom knew one of the families quite well. The telephone rang.

'7412'

'Hi, gorgeous – about picking you up. Is it sensible for me to pick you up at your flat?'

'You must be psychic, Tony. I was just thinking the same thing. What do you suggest?'

'Well presumably you've got a case. Not too heavy is it?'

'No, it's very light actually. I didn't think I'd need a lot of clothes.'

Tony laughed. 'Do you think you could take it down to the tennis club car park and I'll pick you up there? I don't think many of the tennis players know us.'

'No, wait Tony. I've got a better idea. Let me see if I can get hold of Jane and I'll get her to pick me up and take me down there. After all I am supposed to be going away for the weekend with her and I think it would look pretty odd, me walking down the road carrying a case. I'll ring you back in two minutes.'

Liz put the phone down, picked it up again and dialled Jane's number. No reply. 'Oh bum,' Liz said out aloud. She looked up the number of the tennis club and tried that. Fortunately the man that answered knew Jane.

'*Si, Senora* Harrison ees here. *Momento.*'

'Hello, Jane Harrison speaking.'

'Listen Jane, it's me. I can't have Tony picking me up here in the Porsche – the whole world seems to be sitting out on their patios. Could you pick me up and take me down to the tennis club?'

'Yes, sure. You mean now?'

'Yes, if that's OK.'

'No problema. *Hasta la vista.*'

Liz dialled Tony's number.

'Seddon.'

'All systems go. Tennis club car park in five minutes.'

'Wonderful, see you there.'

Liz checked the kitchen equipment. No, nothing was on except the fridge. She picked up her case and walked out on to the patio locking the door behind her.

Jane pulled up outside and Liz got in the passenger seat.

'You really do think things out, don't you?' she said. 'I take endless risks but seem to get away with it – so far anyway.'

Liz explained her thoughts about payment for the hotel and dinner.

'You are amazing,' Jane said. 'A couple of days ago if anyone had suggested I'd be off for a dirty weekend with you and a couple of blokes I'd have thought they were potty. But here we are with every part of the plot planned to the last detail. If there is another war I think you should be made a general.'

'I expect it is because it is my first time and I just couldn't bear anything to go wrong and spoil it all. I'm looking forward to it so much.'

They pulled into the car park and just behind came Tony who parked alongside them.

'Have a good time children,' Jane said. 'Don't do anything I wouldn't do and see you at about nine-thirty in the restaurant.'

89

'Yes,' said Liz, 'and I'll remember to buy you something at El Cortes Ingles. Any idea of what you want?'

'Not really. I'm quite happy to leave it to you.'

Tony took Liz's case and put it in the boot before holding the wide passenger door open for her. He was wearing a pale blue Gabicci shirt, royal blue shorts, long pale blue socks and dark blue docksiders with white trim. The hairs on his brown arms and knees glistened in the sun.

'I don't know if you look better dressed or undressed,' Liz said.

'You look absolutely super, yourself,' Tony replied.

Liz was delighted at the compliment. She was wearing a sleeveless yellow blouse with a touch of blue trim round the collar, pale blue skirt and matching shoes. Her tan had improved over the last few days and the pale colours she was wearing accentuated it.

They pulled out of the car park and Liz sat low in her seat until they had left the complex and were on the road to Murcia with a Barbara Dixon tape murmuring in the background. It was playing 'I Know Him So Well' from Chess and it seemed very apposite. Tony was one of those drivers who seemed to become a part of the car – everything was calm and unhurried yet Liz saw that the speedo was nudging eighty which was appreciably above the speed limit except on a dual carriageway. Tony held out his left hand which Liz clasped to her bosom before kissing it. He smiled at her tenderly but just then had to change gear to overtake so withdrew his hand from hers. Liz was disappointed that he did not offer it back. As if reading her thoughts Tony said, 'I'm afraid I'm one of those people who give one hundred per cent concentration to whatever I'm doing. Sorry.'

'I've noticed, but does it matter what I do?'

'Not a bit, within reason.'

Liz reached across and undid the zip on his shorts. She fumbled with his pants before withdrawing his penis, which almost immediately sprang to life, standing up proud and erect. Liz loosened her seat belt and leant over. She brushed the tip with her lips and caressed it with her tongue.

'I'm going to save that for later. I just wanted to make sure he still liked me.'

'You don't know how much,' Tony said as Liz tucked it back inside his shorts with some difficulty, and pulled up his zip.

They had now joined the main Cartagena/Murcia road and were beginning to climb up the Murcian hills with long views over the coastal plateau towards San Javier and San Pedro de Pinotar with the pale blue of the Mar Menor and beyond that the darker blue of the Mediterranean shimmering in the distance.

Liz snuggled in her seat feeling blissfully happy.

'I just feel so good. I just know this weekend is going to be perfect. What a lucky woman I am.' She sighed with contentment. They were now going down the winding road into the outskirts of Murcia.

'Do you know where this hotel is?' Tony asked.

'No, not exactly but it is in the centre and only a few minutes walk from El Corte Ingles if that is any help. I know the hotel has its own private underground car park so I suggest we go there first and park the car.'

'Good idea. Then we can forget the car and concentrate on each other.'

'Just what I was thinking,' Liz murmured.

They found the hotel without difficulty and parked in the underground car park, having first convinced the attendant that they had a room booked at the hotel. Tony carried their cases up to the reception desk.

'Do you speak English?' Liz asked the man behind the desk.

'*Si*, leetle bit,' he replied.

'You have a double room reserved in the name of Waldren, W-A-L-D-R-E-N.'

'*Si, si*. I have eet. Numero 317. You sign here please and give me *pasaporte*.'

Liz flushed – she had not brought it. It was at the flat.

'Tony, I haven't brought my passport,' she wailed. 'What can we do?'

It's OK, I've got mine.' He reached in his case and produced his passport, which he passed to the clerk.

The clerk looked at it.

'I do not understand, Thees pasaporte is no in name Waldren. Thees pasaporte, eet say Seddon.'

He looked at them from one to the other and Liz blushed furiously. Fortunately Tony came to the rescue.

'*El nombre de esta Senora es Waldren pero me llama Seddon. Comprendes?*' and winked.

'*Si, si. Comprendo. Claro.*' He beamed at them and passed the registration card to Tony.

'You have good time.' It was his turn to wink at Tony, who was now completing the form. The clerk looked at it quickly.

'*Bueno, Entonces.*' He clapped his hands and a young porter came over to take their cases and show them to their room which was tastefully furnished in Spanish style with dark hardwood furniture, twin beds, pleasant pictures and a really nice bathroom with a vanity basin set in marble, matching marble walls and floor, a bath with shower over, WC and bidet.

Tony tipped the porter and they were on their own.

Liz walked up to him, put her arms around his waist and her head against his chest.

'That was so embarrassing,' she said, 'how could I forget my passport? It just never occurred to me. I wonder if Tom took his.'

'Don't worry,' he said tilting her head and kissing her on the nose.

'The clerk doesn't mind. All it means is that the bill will be in my name, but so it should be. I'm not a gigolo.'

'But it can't be,' Liz said with an anguished cry. 'Tom said I must pay it by Barclaycard and he'll be looking for it on his statement.'

'Don't worry,' he said again gently, 'I'll sort it out but not now. I've got better things to do and you are on top of the list.'

He undid her skirt, which fell to the floor, pulled her blouse over her head, undid her bra and kissed each nipple gently, then sank to his knees while he slowly removed her panties. He carried her over to one of the beds, hastily removed his own clothes and lay beside her holding her closely to him, kissing her long and passionately while at the same time rubbing his body against hers. She could feel his hardness against her stomach. 'I want you inside me,' she said, lifting a leg and guiding his penis inside her moist and welcoming vagina. She dropped her leg again holding him tight, then loosened and contracted her muscles.

'This is gorgeous,' Tony said. 'I always knew it would be.' They moved their pelvises slowly in unison and Liz knew that in this position she only had half of him inside her but it was bliss. Everytime we make love this weekend I'll have a bit more she thought. She could feel Tony begin to throb and without a word they both held their bodies still and Liz relaxed her muscles. That would have been too quick. They continued to kiss and fondle each other, stroking each others backs and bottoms and Tony sucked her left breast and licked the nipple until she thought it was as hard as Tony's penis. They started moving together again but this time when Tony began to throb Liz thrust herself against him fiercely and they came

93

together in perfect unison. They lay together with Tony still inside her for quite a long time looking and smiling at each other and sometimes with their eyes closed but never for long as they liked what they saw. Then Tony began to move his body again and Liz could feel him come alive inside her and they abandoned themselves to a frenzied climax which left them both bathed in perspiration.

'Did the earth move, my darling?' Tony said.

'Move? Hasn't Murcia just had an earthquake? You are amazing. God, you're not going to come alive again, are you?'

Tony smiled. 'Not for an hour or two. You've got to do some shopping, haven't you?'

'Yes, but you'll come with me won't you?'

'Of course, I don't want to be apart from you for an instant.' They kissed tenderly and went through to the bathroom together. Tony climbed into the bath first and held out his hand to Liz who stepped in and joined him. He pulled the shower curtain closed, turned on the shower and adjusted the temperature to his satisfaction. He held the shower head in his hand while he sprayed her all over, lifting up her breasts in turn to spray the undersides and parting her legs while he sprayed between them. He passed the shower to Liz for her to spray him while he unwrapped the black Spanish soap and began to soap her all over and when he soaped between her legs it filled her with desire again and she could see his penis begin to quiver. She took the soap from him and began to lather his body and private parts making sure that every part of him received her attention. Tony hung the shower on its hook and they held each other rubbing their slippery soapy bodies together while the clean water rinsed them clean. It was all incredibly sensuous and for two pins they would have gone back to the bedroom and started all over again. But after a final rinse they stood apart, climbed out of the bath and dried each other with the large fluffy towels.

They went back to the bedroom and Liz got the talc and perfume from her overnight bag. They got dressed somewhat reluctantly putting on the same clothes they had worn earlier except that Liz changed her blouse and Tony put on a different shirt and decided to wear long trousers to go shopping.

They walked to El Corte Ingles, which was now thronged with customers, and wandered aimlessly from department to department holding hands and drawing each other's attention to unusual items, which one would be unlikely to find in England. Eventually they decided on a pretty, brightly coloured cotton sun dress for Liz, which she paid for with Tom's money, a really nice leather handbag for Jane, which was about half the price it would have been in Harrods or any other quality shop in England, and some tangerines, grapes and a bottle of champagne for the bedroom. Tony always liked to have some fruit in his bedroom and as there was a fridge the champagne would be nicely chilled when they wanted it. Champagne always made Liz feel sexy and feeling as she did, it seemed like taking coals to Newcastle, but Tony showed no signs of flagging, so why not.

They went back to the hotel another way, looking at the other shops in the centre of Murcia and in a jeweller's Tony saw a brooch which he insisted on buying her. It was not vastly expensive so Liz did not feel embarrassed as she could always say she had bought it herself, but she knew she would treasure it always and remember this weekend in Murcia whenever she wore it. She felt she must buy Tony something and she had noticed in the restaurant the previous evening that he carried his money and credit cards in a cheap plastic wallet supplied by his bank. She found a nice leather wallet with a section for credit cards and Tony seemed thrilled with it, ceremoniously ditching the old plastic one as soon as they left the shop.

They passed a bar and both realised that they had had nothing to eat since breakfast and it was still about three hours until dinner. They went inside and while Liz sat at a table Tony went to the bar and came back with a beer for him, a glass of white wine for Liz and a delicious assortment of *tapas*, including mussels, calamares, stuffed peppers and small pieces of cheese on toast. They ate hungrily but did not have any more so as not to spoil their appetite for dinner.

They returned to the hotel, collected their key and went up to the bedroom, kissing each other hungrily in the lift. Tony put the champagne in the fridge and the fruit on the bedside table.

'What would you like to do now, my love?' he said.

'I think I'd just like us to take all our clothes off and you to hold me in your arms, and we'll see what comes up.'

'I'll be very surprised if something doesn't,' Tony said pulling his shirt over his head and undoing the belt of his trousers. They undressed relatively slowly and folded their clothes neatly on their respective chairs. It was not so warm now and Liz pulled back the bed clothes. They climbed into bed and held each other tenderly, but not with the frenzied passion of a few hours ago. They talked to each other about themselves and filled in most of the gaps from their previous conversation at the cove. Then Tony reached for a tangerine, which he peeled. He placed a segment between his teeth and put his lips to hers. She bit and some juice ran down her chin and Tony licked it off. Then he grabbed a handful of segments and holding his hand above her body squeezed and juice went over her breasts and stomach running into her navel and among her pubic hairs. Again he swooped and licked the juice away. Now it was Liz's turn and she grabbed all that was left of the tangerine and rubbed it hard against his body. She licked the juice away and then massaged his penis with the remainder of the segments and small pieces stuck to it as it began to swell. She gently took each of his balls in her mouth and then she licked him like a cat starting at the top of the balls and running her tongue all the way up his penis while her breasts rested gently on his thighs. He sighed with pleasure and anticipation before she mounted him as she had mounted Tom only a few hours before, but that had been almost clinical. Now she was burning with desire with a fierce energy she could not remember ever feeling with Tom. Was it the foreplay that had excited her so much or did she feel more for Tony than for Tom? If she spent more time with Tony would this incredible lust fade? Would foreplay stop? Why did it stop?

She plunged and reared in a frenzy of sexual stimulation until the climax came and they both shouted out loud and wondered afterwards if anyone had heard them. Not that they cared. A fuck like that deserved a shout. But when had she shouted with Tom? She did not think ever.

When they were first married and could not keep their hands off each other she had been very inhibited, but with Tony she felt she could make love in the High Street and let everyone see her untold joy and exultation.

'Bloody hell,' Tony said. 'I mean bloody marvellous. You are amazing.'

'I don't think it's me. I've never made love like that before – ever. I mean I have in that position but never with that freedom and uncontrolled passion. I just don't have any inhibitions with you. It's wonderful.'

They ate another tangerine in a conventional manner and lay still together, their sweat and Tony's semen mingling among their pubic hairs and on their thighs, but they didn't care and didn't want to move in case it broke the spell. They closed their eyes and probably both dropped off for a while before they were awakened by the telephone. It was pitch dark. Liz fumbled, not sure where the phone or the light switch was. Simultaneously Tony found a light switch and Liz picked up the phone.

'Hello, this is Liz Waldren.'

It's me – Jane. Thought I'd just let you know we've arrived. Didn't interrupt anything did I?'

'No, not at all. In fact it's a good thing you rang as we were both asleep. What time is it?'

'Half eight. Do you want to meet in the bar in half an hour or so and have a drink before dinner?'

'Yes, that sounds great. See you. Bye.'

'That was Jane, Tony. They've arrived. Is that OK to meet them in the bar in half an hour?'

'Yes, why not? Do you think we should have another shower or let them smell what we've been doing?'

Their bed, their bodies, in fact the whole room smelt of them and their wonderful sex, with just a hint of tangerine. Liz had another memory now. Whenever she had a tangerine she would think of Tony and this amazing day of passion in Murcia. A tangerine was never going to be quite the same, ever.

They showered separately this time, Liz having hers while Tony shaved so that she would have time to do her make-up and they were down in the bar in little over half an hour. James and Jane were already there, the inevitable gin and tonics on the table in front of them. James rose to his feet.

'Hello Liz, and you must be Tony Seddon.' He held out his hand to Tony. 'This is Jane, my tennis partner – for want of a better description.' Tony shook hands with them both. 'What can I get you both to drink?'

A waiter came over to take the order and James and Jane ordered two more gin and tonics for themselves.

98

'Liz, while I think of it,' Jane said, 'Didn't you tell Tom and Gilbert the room was booked in your name?'

'Yes, why? It is, isn't it?'

'Well, no, it's not. When I asked for Mrs Waldren's room they said "They no have room in name Waldren. Only English people called Seddon" so naturally I asked them to put me through but thinking about it, it could be a bit tricky as and when Tom or Gilbert phone, don't you think?'

Liz suddenly felt cold and saw goose pimples come up on her arm. 'Oh, my God. I never thought. You see the room was in my name but I forgot to bring my passport but Tony had his so obviously they've changed the name. And of course you filled in the registration form, didn't you Tony? Oh, my God! Tom's bound to ring and if they say the same to him as they said to you – what can we do?'

Tony rose swiftly from his chair.

'Leave it to me. I'm sure I can sort this out.'

'Would you like me to come with you?' Liz said.

'No, its OK thanks. A bit of man to man chat is called for I think.'

Liz felt slightly sick and had an awful sinking feeling in her stomach. What if Tom had already rung the hotel? If the receptionist had said the same to him as to Jane he would know she must be with Tony and he could be driving to Murcia at this very moment. And if she were with Tony, Gilbert would be equally suspicious of Jane. She would hardly have come along just to play goose-berry. She'd landed them both in it. Again she shivered. 'Oh Jane, I'm so sorry. I thought I'd been so clever and in fact I've really messed things up, for both of us. I just never thought about a passport. It's so rare Tom and I stay in an hotel abroad. In fact I very much doubt if he has taken his either.'

'Don't worry so much, Liz. Tony is sorting the name business out,' Jane said.

'But what if one of them has phoned already? They could be on their way here now. They could walk into this bar any minute,' Liz wailed.

'Christ, I hadn't thought of that,' Jane said. 'Where's that bloody gin and tonic? I really need another one now.'

At that moment Tony came back grinning from ear to ear.

'All fixed,' he said. 'It's amazing what a couple of thousand pesetas will do in Spain. The night receptionist has just come on duty and any call for either of you will come straight through to our room. Hope there aren't too many though. Could put me right off my stroke.'

'Oh, Tony. How can you joke at a time like this?' Liz cried. 'If this chap has only just come on duty you don't know if any calls were made earlier, do you? I mean Tom or Gilbert could have phoned ages ago straight after their golf. They could walk in here any minute.'

'Hadn't thought of that, I must admit, still better now than an hour or two ago.' Tony smiled at Liz again. 'Don't worry – try and relax. I don't know what we can do now in any case.' Liz stood up.

'Well I do. I'm going to ring Tom. I couldn't eat a mouthful of food feeling as I do now and at least then we'll know. Can I have the key? I'll go to the bedroom.'

Tony handed over the bedroom key. 'Would you like me to come with you?' he asked.

'Why? Do you want to have a word with Tom too?' Liz said bitterly, striding off towards the lift. Tony looked uncomfortable. Jane leant forward and put her hand on his arm.

'Stay where you are, Tony. Liz is upset. You see she has never done anything like this before and her planning has been meticulous. Now because she didn't think to bring her passport she feels her marriage is threatened and of course her relationship with you. If she gets through to

100

Tom and neither of them has phoned she'll be fine. Enjoy your drink.'

'I do hope you're right,' Tony said. 'She's such a super person. I would hate her to get hurt.'

When Liz got to the bedroom she sat down on the unused bed and picked up the instructions for the use of the telephone. Thank God: they were in three languages including English. She obtained an outside line and dialled the number of the Parador.

Her dress felt clammy against her skin from her nervous perspiration and she did not like looking at the rumpled bed when she was trying to speak to Tom. She moved over to that one and sat down again.

'*Senor* Waldren, *por favor*,' she said when the hotel answered.

'*Momento*,' the telephonist said. 'There ees no reply from hees room,' he said a few seconds later.

'Could you try the restaurant?' Liz said. 'It's really is most urgent.'

The seconds ticked away and Liz felt herself break into a sweat again.

'Hello,' Tom's voice boomed down the telephone. 'Who's that?'

'It's me darling,' Liz said brokenly. 'I'm sorry. Have I interrupted your dinner? I just had to speak to you.'

'What's the trouble, old girl? You sound awful. Are you all right?'

'Oh yes, Tom, I'm all right. I just had to speak to you as I said. Did you have a nice game? Is the hotel nice?' The words came tumbling out. Tom, on the other hand, spoke very slowly.

'Yes, we had a super game and the course really is all its cracked up to be – and yes, the hotel is fine. Now what is all this about? The waiter said it was most urgent.'

'Oh Tom, I'm so sorry. I'm just being stupid but I just

101

had to speak to you. I love you so much. I'm all right now. Have a lovely weekend. Jane sends her love. Take care and play well tomorrow.'

'OK,' Tom said. 'You're sure you're all right?'

'Yes Tom, honestly, I'm fine. Now go back and enjoy your dinner. Bye darling. Love you lots.'

Liz put the phone down. She was still shaking slightly and her dress still felt clammy. She took all her clothes off and went through to the bathroom. I'll just have another quick shower she thought. The hot water made her feel better. Thank goodness I brought a spare blouse she thought. As she was towelling herself down there was a knock on the door.

'Who is it?' she called.

'It's me, Tony.'

She walked over and turned the catch on the door.

'I'm sorry. I don't think I'm cut out to be an adultress.'

'I wouldn't say that, but what happened? Did you speak to Tom?'

'Oh yes. I've spoken to him. It's all right. He hadn't phoned, but Tony, I was so frightened.'

Tony put his arms round her and held her to him, stroking her hair. 'It's all right. I understand. I think it is because I am the first in your life since Tom that makes our relationship so special. If you were the sort of woman who had affairs regularly, I don't expect I'd feel anything like the same way about you. You are so sweet, and so very special.'

He continued to hold her, stroking her hair and gently kissing her forehead and eyes.

'What about our lovely dinner?' Liz cried. 'It must be ages after nine thirty.'

'It's all right,' Tony replied gently. 'This is Spain. The table is ready when we are and Jane and James seem quite happy tucking into their gin and tonics – or do I mean gins and tonic?'

'Yes, I'm afraid they are a bit dipso, aren't they? Will you wait while I get dressed? I'm afraid I can't wear my dress, it's soaking.'

'Yes, of course I'll wait. Just as long as you like.'

Tony picked up the dress and hung it in the wardrobe. He then made the bed and sat in the armchair watching her finish getting dressed and putting on her make-up.

'Sorry it just has to be a blouse and skirt. I wanted to dress up for you tonight.'

'You look wonderful in anything – and nothing – you've undressed quite beautifully as well. Are you feeling better now?'

'Yes, I'm fine. I'm hungry too. Let's go or those two will be completely stoned.'

They locked the door, took the lift and walked slowly into the bar.

'It's OK,' Liz said. 'I must have sounded a bit odd because I was in such a panic and to start with they couldn't find Tom so I was fearing the worst, but neither of them have rung so we can relax. Shall we go and eat? I'm starving.'

They went through to the olde worlde restaurant with its beamed ceiling and warm pale gold walls with matching table linen. They admired the array of fine oil paintings on display. There was no suggestion that they were late although it was now after half past ten and Liz reflected how different it would be in England. They had a splendid meal, beautifully served and they particularly enjoyed the '78 Gran Reserva Rioja that Tony had chosen to go with the main course. Its deep red colour and slight oaky flavour was really warming and Liz felt human again. As they were ordering coffee the head waiter came over.

'Telephone for *Senora* Kennedy,' he said.

Jane went through to the reception desk, a little

unsteadily, and came back a few minutes later smiling broadly.

'That was Gilbert, needless to say. He said Tom had had this rather odd call from you and were we all right. I said just great,' she squeezed James's thigh, 'well I suppose time will tell. Anyway I had this brilliant wheeze. I said we had been propositioned by this Spanish waiter who had suggested that he came to our room later and would we like him to bring his friend and that this had upset you.'

'Gosh, that's brilliant, Jane,' Liz said. 'I've been racking my brains to think what might have upset me, but that is perfect. I'm sure it would have upset me, too.'

'Oh, I don't know – I mean if we had been here on our own. I think I'd have been happy to give it a whirl. Spaniards are supposed to be pretty good, I'm told.'

James made as if to leave. 'Well, if I'm not wanted.'

'Of course you're wanted. I'm only teasing.'

They all had Carlos Primeros with their coffee, except Liz who ordered a Cuarenta y Tres, which she always enjoyed, especially when it was served with crushed ice.

They went up to their rooms soon after midnight and as they were walking along the corridor to their room Tony said, 'Your marriage is very important to you, isn't it?'

'Oh Tony, I don't know. You just drive me wild with desire like no man ever has in my life and when I'm in bed with you I can think of nothing else but . . . Yes, I suppose it must be mustn't it? This evening proved it. You see Tom and I have been together for so long and there are the children and Jean is getting married next year and nothing must spoil that, and then there's the house and lots of friends at home and at the same time I'm crazy about you. I don't know. I mean you're everything Tom isn't. You flatter me and you just have to touch me and . . . I don't want to be disloyal to Tom. We have good sex too but its – I don't know – mechanical does not seem the right word but it's not new. I don't get surprised. Technically it's probably good but it's not innovative. We have very little foreplay and we never use tangerines,' Liz giggled. 'Will you kiss me please?'

Tony took her in his arms and kissed her long and tenderly, his tongue probing her mouth and she could feel him begin to harden against her as she rubbed her breasts against his chest and thrust her pelvis against his. She pulled herself away.

'That's enough of that. I'm ready for my bed.'

Tony unlocked the bedroom door.

'To sleep, perchance to screw,' he misquoted.

They undressed quickly and cleaned their teeth. Liz got into the unused bed and lay on her side. She felt Tony climb in behind her and he cupped her right breast in his right hand, gently rubbing her nipple with his thumb. She could feel herself getting roused yet again but she made no move. Tony was rubbing his pelvis gently against her bottom and she could feel him harden between her cheeks.

'Do you think there's room for one inside?' he murmured.

He drew away from her slightly and then she could feel the tip of his penis probing the lips of her vagina. He moved very slowly, continuing to caress her right breast and nipple. The sensation was exquisite and she could feel herself approaching orgasm already. Reading her reactions perfectly Tony whispered, 'Don't hold back – let it come – I'll catch up later.'

Obediently Liz climaxed but Tony did not stop his slow languorous movements. He moved his right hand slowly down her stomach to her pubic hair and gently pushed his hand against the inside of her thigh and as she lifted her leg slightly she felt his finger enter the mouth of her vagina and begin rubbing against her clitoris. The sensation was

105

unbelievable and in almost no time she achieved simultaneous internal and external orgasms, but still Tony carried on, his movements now a little quicker and his thrusts a little deeper.

'Roll over on your stomach and then up on your knees,' he said, matching her movements exactly and nuzzling her right ear. Now he thrust hard and deeply and she could feel every millimetre of him. They climaxed together with another great cry of exultation before collapsing together, but with Tony still inside her.

'That was wonder . . .' Liz started to say but fell asleep before finishing the sentence, completely content and satisfied.

8

Liz woke up with a start next morning, wondering where she was, and remembering snuggled up against Tony's warm body.

'Have you slept well, my love?' Tony asked, without opening his eyes.

'Mm, must have, I've only just woken up. You were fantastic last night. I just went out like a light. What's the time?'

Tony reached for his watch. 'Just after seven.'

'Do you want to try and go back to sleep or shall I make a coffee, or should we have the champagne?'

'No, I'm sure I wouldn't go back to sleep, especially with you all wide-eyed and beautiful. Coffee would be lovely. We'll save the champagne for a little later.'

Liz ran water into the kettle and while it was coming to the boil she peeled two tangerines and brought them over to Tony with a few grapes.

'Do you mind if I ring Tom in a few minutes?'

'No, of course not. Would you like me to go through to the bathroom?'

'Good Lord, no. It's just to reassure him after my panic yesterday and to see if they have decided to stay at El Saler tonight. I forgot to ask last night and it would be nice to know, don't you think?' Liz smiled meaningfully at him.

'Certainly would. Tom is a lot bigger than me and I don't fancy a fight with a jealous husband with right on his side.'

'He's not bigger everywhere I can assure you.' Liz said as she passed him his cup of coffee. She sat on the side of the bed while they ate the fruit and sipped the coffee. Liz was surprised that she did not feel embarrassed sitting there in the nude. She had always imagined that with any man other than Tom she would feel ashamed of the droop in her breasts and her small spare tyre which appeared after Peter was born and had never completely disappeared despite lots of exercises. Children have a lot to answer for she had often thought – not just their cost but the pain, the stretching of the muscles, the worries, the anxieties, the compromises about holidays and theatres, even television and yet she knew she would have hated not to have had children. With any luck she would be a grandmother in a year or two and she really looked forward to that. She loved small children and the idea of having access to children but being able to get rid of them when one had had enough appealed to her enormously. Perhaps when they got a bit older she and Tom would take them to La Manga for a holiday, but that would put the kibosh on anything like this weekend. But this was a one off. It had to be. She wasn't naturally a deceitful person and she knew she would not be able to lie to Tom on a long term basis. No, this weekend had been meant to happen. Everything had conspired to make it possible. But she must have been wanting it to happen subconsciously. She had deliberately started a conversation with Tony only three, four days ago and now she seemed to know him so well and their bodies fused together as one.

She remembered discussing unfaithfulness at a Ladies' Circle coffee morning years ago and she had been surprised how many of her friends had been propositioned at some time or another, in some cases many times but it had never happened to her. Why was that? She did not feel that she was any less attractive than most of the other wives. She had discussed it with Tom, she remembered. He had said it was nothing to do with attractiveness but how a woman looked at a man. Nothing had to be said but there was a certain boldness in the way a woman looked at a man when she was ready to have an affair and the vibes were instantly recognised by the man.

'Did you think you would go to bed with me, when I talked to you that day on the balcony of the club?' Liz asked.

'I'm not as bigheaded as that,' Tony replied. 'I know I thought this is an attractive woman who is not getting the attention she should and then when you responded so eagerly to my suggestion of a golf lesson, I thought I had a chance. I never dreamt that it would be as wonderful as it has.'

He put his hand on her thigh and began to caress it, his fingers running through her pubic hair.

'None of that – I must ring Tom and I must concentrate on what I'm saying.'

She moved over to the other bed while she dialled the number of the Parador and got put through to Tom's room.

'Hello darling, this is your early morning call,' she said. Tom laughed.

'Hello, old girl. You sound better. Are you OK now? I nearly rang back last night but after Gilbert had spoken to Jane he explained that you'd been upset by some randy Spanish waiter. You didn't have any more trouble did you?'

'No, I'm fine. Jane was marvellous. Is it a nice day in Valencia?'

'Yes, it looks great. I'm just going down to breakfast as we're off at nine.'

'Do you think you will be coming back this evening?'

'I don't know really. We'll probably discuss it at breakfast. It doesn't matter does it? You and Jane are going back to La Manga anyway, aren't you?'

'Oh yes, we'll probably have a bit more of a look round Murcia this morning and leave lunch-timish I should think. We might go back via Orihuela, it's supposed to be an interesting old town.'

'Fine. See you when I see you then. Must go. Take care, old thing.'

Liz put the phone down. 'Oh, bum,' she said.

'Left it open, has he? Can't say I blame him. Still we've got all day together haven't we? Let's make sure we don't waste it.' Tony got up, went over to the mini-bar and got out the bottle of champagne and a couple of glasses. He deftly removed the cork and poured the sparkling liquid.

'With or without orange juice?'

'Oh, without I think. Champagne breakfast! What bliss!'

He brought the glasses over, dipped his finger in one and pressed it to her lips. He kissed her hungrily licking the champagne from her lips and chin. Soon they were covering themselves with the pale golden liquid and licking it from each other's bodies. And then they were making love again, rolling across the bed first with Tony on top, then sideways, then with Liz on top at the same time kissing each other's ears, necks, faces, indeed anywhere they could reach with their probing tongues. When they neared climax they lay still, holding each other before starting again. It seemed to go on for ages until with one accord they decided to come and Tony exploded deep inside her. They lay still.

'What are we going to do today then?' Tony asked.

Anything you like as long as we do it together. Perhaps it would be nice to go to Orihuela sometime as I mentioned it to Tom.'

'Mm – probably better check what Jane and James are doing. Can't have you knowing all about the place and Jane not having a clue.'

'Yes, that's true. I'll give her a ring.'

Liz picked up the phone again and dialled. It rang several times.

'Yes,' Jane said.

'Hi, Jane,' Liz said brightly.

'Christ, it's you. I'll ring you back.'

Liz replaced the phone. 'I think I interrupted something,' She said.

About ten minutes later the phone rang.

'Sorry about that,' Liz said. 'Either you started later than us or are doing it more often.'

Jane laughed.

'I shouldn't think it's more often. I reckon Tony's a lot fitter than James. Still, you're not too bad, are you darling,' she added as an aside. 'Anyway what's the problem?'

'No problem. Just wondered what your plans were. I've spoken to Tom and got absolutely nowhere. They may be back this evening or they may not.'

'Typical bloody men. Still we can ring the Parador about seven can't we? Ask to speak to one of them and if they are not there we put our clothes on and don the welcoming smile. If they are there we say how much we are missing them and have another wild night of passion. Dunno if James could cope actually. He looks shattered. How's Tony? Have you worn him out?'

'Don't think so. He still seems full of beans. What are you going to do today?'

'Oh, sorry. I didn't answer that question. There's a mixed tournament at the Club this afternoon so we've got to be back there for two. Can't see us doing any good, looking at my old chap but maybe he'll get his second wind.'

111

'Oh, OK. It's just I said to Tom we might go back via Orihuela.'

'Ori what? Well you do what you like, you can always give me some snippet of information about the place when you get back to La Manga. Gilbert won't be very interested anyway, if I know him. Have a good day and come to the tennis club when you get back. We'll be there all afternoon.'

'Right. Good luck in the tennis. Bye.'

Tony and Liz had a leisurely shower and dressed slowly, sipping what was left of the champagne. They both felt totally relaxed in mind and body. They walked down to breakfast holding hands. Afterwards they packed their few clothes and both took a long lingering look round the bedroom not wishing to forget a single feature of a room which had witnessed what they felt was the ultimate in love making.

'Remember, I've got to pay the bill,' Liz said.

'I am remembering but I find it very embarrassing. I feel like some cheap gigolo.'

'Don't be silly,' Liz squeezed his hand. 'Don't ever think I haven't had my money's worth.'

'No, I think we've both had that but Tom hasn't and presumably it's his money. It makes it even worse.'

'Don't be a silly goose – you can give me some cash sometime if you feel that badly, but it's quite unnecessary.'

They checked the bill and found dinner was not on it. This had been put on James's bill. Tony sorted this out and Liz presented her Barclaycard.

'You come again soon,' the receptionist said as he handed her back her card and the receipt.

'Oh, I do hope so,' replied Liz looking at Tony and giving him an almost imperceptible wink.

They went down to the car and drove round Murcia for

an hour or so before taking the road to Orihuela where the old part of the town stands on a narrow strip of land between a small mountain and the river Segura. Tony parked the car near the centre and they walked round the town holding hands. They admired the cathedral, which dated back to the fourteenth century, and its fine Renaissance portal. The cloisters were cool out of the hot sun, but they did not go inside the church as Mass was being celebrated. Feeling thirsty they looked for somewhere to have a glass of wine and some *tapas* but nothing appealed to them in the town centre and the river was very dirty and gave off a most unpleasant smell. They decided to look for somewhere in the country and were soon on the road to San Pedro de Pinotar on the edge of the Mar Menor.

'I'm so happy,' said Liz. 'I just wish this weekend would never end.'

'Me too but I also keep wondering how and when we are going to see each other again after you go back to England on Tuesday. This can't just be a one-off, can it?'

'Oh Tony. I do hope not. We'll have to make plans. Perhaps when Tom goes off to one of his golf things we could meet. We must be able to work something out. And you can ring me. Tom has always left the house by eight thirty and I never go out before nine thirty so that's a good time. And I'll get the dates when Tom is away.' Liz squeezed his arm. 'I've got to be able to look forward to feeling you inside me again. Apart from that I've spoken to Tom about me coming to La Manga on my own and you could be here at the same time. Just imagine. . . .'

They drove back to La Manga slowly, stopping every now and again to admire a view or building, standing with their arms round each other and sometimes kissing tenderly. They found a nice restaurant, set well back from the road and sat outside under a large umbrella while they ate their *tapas* and drank their wine. Around them were

113

lots of Spanish families having enormous amounts to eat and Tony explained that Sunday lunchtime was the time whole families got together and the more well-to-do went to restaurants, while the poorer people probably had a large paella or *cocido* at home.

When they got back to the complex they went straight to the tennis club, as arranged, and Liz went off to see if she could find Jane so that she could put her case in her car. Sure enough Jane and James were on the verandah with gin and tonics in front of them.

'You haven't won already, have you?' Liz asked.

'No such luck,' Jane replied. 'We both played appallingly badly. Still, I've no regrets, it was worth it.'

Liz told them a little about Orihuela and what they had seen on the way back and then borrowed the keys to Jane's car. They agreed that Jane would come up to Liz's apartment at about seven and would try and ring Gilbert from there. Liz put her case in Jane's car and returned the key to her.

'See you about seven, then. Will you come too, James?'

'Yes, I'd like to. Thanks.'

Liz went back to the Porsche where Tony was sitting listening to one of his tapes.

'Come up to the flat as soon as you can,' Liz said. Things felt a bit flat now that they were back and Liz wondered if they would recapture the magic of Murcia.

'Try and stop me. I'll just park at the hotel, put my case in my room and I'll walk up.'

'Great. Would you like a cup of tea?'

Tony laughed. 'Sounds silly out here doesn't it but yes, I would absolutely love a cup of tea, especially made by an English woman.'

'Good, I'm dying for a cuppa. See you in about a quarter of an hour then.'

Liz looked at her watch. Six o'clock. This was really

nice. They would have nearly an hour together on their own whatever else happened, and hopefully the men would decide to stay another night at El Saler.

As soon as she got to the flat she got out two cups and saucers and found some biscuits. She put them on a tray and put the kettle on. What a lovely day it has been, she thought. It started with champagne in bed and now good old-fashioned tea and biscuits. Would they have them in a conventional way she wondered? She heard footsteps on the patio. Tony had been quick. She turned expectantly. Tom's burly figure loomed in the doorway.

'Surprise, surprise,' he boomed. 'Expecting someone?' he said noticing the tea cups on the tray.

'Gosh. No, well I mean, yes, possibly. Jane said she might come up for a cuppa so I put out two cups, just in case,' Liz stammered. 'Would you like a cup?'

'Good idea, old girl. Keep me off the booze a bit longer.'

What was she to do? Tony would be here any minute and he certainly would not be expecting to see Tom. How could she warn him?

'Why don't you go out on the patio and I'll bring it out to you as soon as it is made?' she said.

At least if he were outside Tony would see him and would probably just wave and carry on walking past the flat. Tom went to the door and stopped.

'Better make room for it first.' He retraced his steps and went up to the bathroom. If Tony came now how could she explain it? She went out on to the patio. Tony was just walking down the hill. He was about fifty yards away. She couldn't call out. Tom would hear. She heard the flush of the cistern and then Tom's footsteps crossing the bedroom. Now Tony had seen her. He quickened his pace. Liz wanted to signal for him to turn round and go back but Tom would see her through the big window as he came across the lounge.

115

'Tom's just got back from Valencia,' she half croaked, half shouted. 'We're going to have a cup of tea. Will you join us?'

'Who are you talking to?' Tom said as he came out on to the patio. 'Oh, if it isn't Tony Seddon – well fancy that,' he added sarcastically.

'Hello Liz, Tom,' Tony said. 'That's very nice of you. I'd love to if it's no trouble.'

'Of course not,' Liz said, 'Sit down. I'll just go and get another cup.'

Tom and Tony sat down.

'And what brings you to Miradores this Sunday afternoon?' Tom growled.

'Oh, I had to rearrange a golf lesson with some people in 390 and it was such a lovely afternoon I thought I'd walk back the long way round,' Tony replied easily.

'Hmph. Thought you were away deep sea fishing today. That's what you told me.'

'Y-yes, that's right. It was a great disappointment actually. We set off this morning as arranged but the engine started playing up and we decided to pack it in at about eleven, so here I am.'

'Hmph,' Tom snorted again. 'Didn't think I'd be here at this time though, did you? Thought I'd be in bloody Valencia well out of harm's way.'

'I hadn't really thought about it but now you mention it I suppose I would. You intended playing all day at El Saler, didn't you?'

'You know bloody well I did.'

Liz came through from the living room.

'Would either of you like a biscuit?' she said brightly.

'No, we don't want a bloody biscuit,' Tom replied, 'and I think you had better go, Seddon. It seems more than a coincidence that you should turn up when you did. Liz and I have got some straight talking to do.'

116

Tony stood up. 'As you wish. I'm just sorry that I decided to walk back this way. I could just as easily have gone the other.'

'But that wouldn't have taken you past this flat would it?' Tom growled. 'Goodbye Seddon. By the way what's the name of the people in 390?'

'Rogers, Bruce and Sheila Rogers,' Tom replied. 'Goodbye Liz, thank you for the offer of tea.'

He walked back up the hill towards the car park and Liz thought he'll be walking past 390. If there are people there called Bruce and Sheila Rogers he can probably square things with them with his charm. She just hoped the same thought was not going through Tom's mind.

'Sit down, Liz,' Tom said, 'and tell me what the hell all this is about. You were expecting him weren't you? How did that happen?'

'Oh, Tom.' Liz wailed, 'Don't try and make such a big issue out of it. Yes, I was expecting him but it was no big deal. When Jane and I got back from Murcia we went straight to the tennis club and Tony was there – don't ask me why because I don't know. Anyway we were talking about having a drink and although Jane was all for having one of her inevitable gin and tonics it was a bit early for me, and Tony said that what he would really like was a nice cup of tea. That appealed to me too but you know how awful the tea is here so I said why didn't he come up to the flat and I'd make him one here. Then like a fool I said he should leave his car at the hotel and walk up because if he left his car here, someone was bound to notice it and well – you know the rest.'

'And why shouldn't he have his car up here if it's all so bloody innocent, or was it just tea for starters? And what about this cock-and-bull story with the people in 390?'

'I don't know anything about the people in 390. He might have just said that to try and help me out but whatever has got into you Tom? You're not usually this jealous and suspicious. It's because of your attitude regarding Tony that I suggested it. I thought someone might tell you that Tony's car had been up here while you were away and you would immediately think the worst. I just didn't want that sort of hassle, but I seem to have got it anyway.'

'Mm, all very plausible,' Tom said, 'but I'm damned glad I was here. I don't trust that bloke. He's too charming by half. None of the fellows I know trust him, not with women anyway.'

'Well you don't have to worry with me,' Liz put her hand on Tom's arm. 'Maybe with someone who is unhappily married but I've got you. We're happy aren't we? I'm sure it would just have been a cup of tea and if he'd suggested anything more, which I doubt, I'd have sent him packing.'

Liz could hardly believe it was her saying this. She felt she knew how St Peter must have felt when he denounced Jesus. But she must protect her marriage. That was vital.

'How come you are back so early anyway?' she asked.

'Oh, we'd no sooner finished our morning round and it started peeing down. According to the local forecast it was going to carry on for a few hours so as Harold was tired and Margaret and Sue were bored, not being able to do anything outside, we decided to come back.' Tom put his arm round Liz's waist. 'How about showing me how much you've missed me then?'

Liz looked at her watch.

'Oh darling, I'm sorry but Jane will be coming up anytime. She's still got my case in her car and I asked her to pop in for a drink – in fact she's coming with that chap she plays a lot of tennis with – James someone – he was at the club as well. I don't expect they will stay long especially when Jane knows Gilbert is back. I wonder if he's been down to the tennis club.'

118

'I doubt that very much,' Tom replied, 'I think Gilbert's feelings about this James are even stronger than mine about Tony. I wish you hadn't asked him actually. It's as if we are encouraging this relationship, if that is what it is, and I'd hate Gilbert to think that.'

Tom went up to the bedroom to unpack the few things he had taken to El Saler while Liz cleared away the tea things.

'I got a lovely sun dress with your money,' Liz called out.

'I'll show it to you when Jane brings my case. She bought a super leather handbag which I must say was jolly good value.' Liz was beginning to feel a little more comfortable and relaxed. Tom seemed to be acting relatively normally now. As long as Jane didn't say anything to re-arouse his suspicions. She must keep an eye out for the car and she could go out and meet them and warn them, if they didn't know already, that Gilbert and Tom were back. That would seem quite normal. Jane was her friend and Tom did not know James so what more natural than that she should walk a few steps to meet them.

Soon afterwards Jane's red Seat drove by with Jane waving cheerily in the general direction of Tom and Liz's apartment. Liz went out on to the patio and walked a few yards towards them as they came down the hill with James carrying her case.

'The chaps are back,' Liz said *sotto voce*.

'Christ, really!' Jane said. 'Why? When?'

'Can't go into that now – just be careful what you say. OK?'

They entered the flat and Liz saw that Tom had already poured himself a large Scotch, which was ominous.

'Evening Jane. I'm not going to suggest you stay for long as I'm sure Gilbert would like to see you – on your own – but I daresay you'd like a quick gin and tonic.'

119

'Yes, that would be lovely Tom. Do you mind if I use your phone?' Without waiting for an answer she picked up the receiver and dialled her own flat.

'Hello darling. What a lovely surprise! I had a couple of sets of tennis after we got back and I've just popped into Tom and Liz's and am going to have a very quick drink and I'll be with you. I've only just this minute found out that you are back. In fact Liz and I planned to ring your hotel about now to see if you were still there. See you in a few minutes. Bye.' She replaced the receiver.

'Oh, I'm sorry. This is James. Tom Waldren – James Hislop.'

'Evening,' Tom grunted. 'Drink?'

'I'm very pleased to meet you Tom. I have had the pleasure of meeting your charming wife. A gin and tonic would be super. Thank you.'

'What do you want Liz?'

'I'll just have an *agua*, thank you darling.'

They went out on to the patio to enjoy the view of the sun setting behind the hills.

'When did you get back here, then?' Tom asked.

Liz and Jane looked at each other waiting to see who would answer.

'I think it was about four, wasn't it Jane?' Liz said.

'Yes, it must have been. We went straight to the tennis club. James was there so we decided to have a knock and you came back up here, Liz. Well, you must know the rest I guess, Tom.'

'It's good to have them back isn't it Jane?' Liz said brightly.

'Oh yes. Great. Still it was fun in Murcia wasn't it? We had a marvellous dinner and even a proposition as well. I suppose you heard about that, Tom?'

'Yes. Gilbert told me. Bloody cheek I call it. Did you go to Orihuela?'

'Oh yes. Yes, we did,' Liz replied. 'It's only about twenty miles from Murcia but we didn't stay long. The most interesting things are the churches and, of course, they were holding mass when we were there so we couldn't go inside. I'd like to go back one day during the week to have a good look at the cathedral.' Jane stood up.

'Well I must go and see my old chap. Are you coming James? I can drop you off at the club if you like.'

James also stood up. 'If you are sure that is no trouble. Thank you very much for the drink. It was very nice meeting you, Tom.'

He held out his hand to Tom who appeared to ignore it and they went up the hill towards their car.

'What a bloody drip,' said Tom when they were out of earshot. 'I can understand Gilbert being upset – it's a real insult to him if Jane spends much time with that ponce.'

'Well he's certainly not my type,' Liz said putting her arm round Tom, 'but then I've got you. Shall I show you how much I've missed you now?'

Tom shrugged her off. 'I'm not in the mood now. I'm going down to the club for a drink. I want to see what time I'm off tomorrow in the Stableford, anyway.'

He left the flat without another word and Liz waited for the car to drive past before picking up the phone and dialling Tony's room.

'Seddon.'

'God, wasn't that awful? I'm so sorry. I thought Tom was going to hit you at one time.'

'Yes, it wasn't a good scene was it? Anyway I bumped into the Rogers and they will back me up if Tom checks with them. You don't think he'll ring the hotel do you?'

'No, I shouldn't think so, his Spanish is too bad. I suppose if he met someone who is fluent he might ask him to but I don't think he would confess his suspicions to a stranger, he's far too macho for that. And don't worry about the Rogers. I had to confess I'd invited you up for a cup of tea. I couldn't explain two tea cups on the tray when he walked in.'

'Oh God. I hadn't thought of that. You poor old love. You did have all your clothes on, did you, and you hadn't put the tea tray by the bed?'

'No it wasn't as bad as that. Initially I said that I thought Jane might come up for a cuppa but after you had gone I had to admit I had invited you, because, of course, Jane was coming up, but a bit later, and with James, so that would never have worked. Anyway hopefully I convinced him that it was all totally innocent and that in any case I'd have sent you packing if you'd tried anything. Oh, Tony, I felt so awful and such a hypocrite.'

'Don't worry. I'm sure you said all the right things but I am glad you phoned because if I bump into him I might well get another grilling. Did you have an explanation for my cock and bull story about the Rodgers?'

'I said you must have just said that to try and protect me as he was in such a foul mood and acting so suspiciously.'

'Fine. Why had I walked up from the hotel and not given you a lift to your flat in my car?'

'Oh, that was my suggestion in case anyone saw us arrive in your car and told Tom. It would have looked a bit funny wouldn't it? As if we'd been away for a dirty weekend together or something like that?'

'Yes, that sounds good. Now, when am I going to see you again?'

'Oh Tony. I don't know. You know I'd love to but I don't think I dare arrange another golf lesson. Tom has gone down to the club now and after a few more drinks he will probably be more belligerent than ever and we fly back on Tuesday, as you know.'

'I wasn't really thinking of a golf lesson, you know. I was thinking much more on the lines of the two of us together all on our own.'

'I'd love it, if you think it's safe. I know Tom is playing in the Stableford tomorrow morning.' Liz added doubtfully.

'That's wonderful. Not much more than twelve hours from now. I've got lessons in the morning from ten but I'm free before then. I tell you what. I'll check Tom's starting time. It's bound to be early with his handicap. I'll watch him drive off and then come straight up to your flat. How does that sound?'

'It sounds absolutely wonderful. I can hardly wait. I don't normally get dressed for breakfast when Tom has an early start so I'll be ready and waiting.'

'Sound like BURMA.'

'BURMA. What's that?'

'What we used to write on the backs of envelopes. Be Undressed and Ready My Angel.' They both laughed. *'Hasta luego. Te quiero.'*

Liz put the phone down and sighed with relief. At least she was going to see Tony again and hold him in her arms.

She tidied the flat and began to prepare supper. Better be something cold she thought as she couldn't be sure what time Tom would be back. Could be half an hour or two hours.

She had some cold chicken in the fridge and prepared a salad. She also got some cheese out and put it on the work top as Tom never liked cheese straight out of the fridge. He always said it had no taste if it was too cold. She sat down and tried to read her book but she couldn't concentrate. She wanted Tony so much but she still wanted her marriage. She must be careful. Would Tony ring her when they got back to England as she had suggested? He had never said how much she meant to him. He certainly enjoyed making love to her but was that enough? Perhaps he had someone in Norfolk with whom he enjoyed sex just as much. Yet he was so tender and thoughtful when they made love. He seemed to find her climaxes more important than his own. She did hope that this was not just a holiday affair, but even if it were it had been worth it. The excitement, the thrill, even the worry but all these sensations had made her come alive. They had barely been away from La Manga for twenty four hours but never in her life had she made love so often in such a short period of time and the quality of the love making had been so sensational. If she could just see Tony as much as once a month in England, even if it were only for a drink but would they be satisfied with that. Where would they meet? What risks would they have to take? Would they be found out? She tried to read her book again and got on a little better but she still would not have liked an English test on what she had just read.

She heard footsteps on the patio. It was Tom. Not too late after all.

'I've just seen lover boy again, in the 37th, and those Rogers people he was talking about.' Liz could feel her heart pounding. Please God there had not been a scene.

'Apparently he had seen them about changing a time so part of what he said was true even if he was not totally honest. I still can't see why he couldn't have said you had asked him up for a cup of tea if it was all so bloody innocent.'

'Oh, Tom. It was your attitude. I'm sure he would have done normally but you were being so aggressive and as you say he had to be up here anyway, he probably just said the first thing that came into his head.'

'Mm, maybe. Anyway we got talking about your golf and he seems to think that you could become quite a reasonable player and is keen that you carry on with it so

124

we've arranged for you to have another lesson at three-thirty tomorrow. He wants me to come along too so that I can see what he's taught you and then I should be able to take on from there, to a large extent.' Liz sighed with relief.

'That would be great. I never thought I would enjoy golf but I have really enjoyed my lessons with Tony and can certainly hit the ball better than I expected. Tony is so encouraging too – he keeps pointing out people on the practice ground, a lot of whom are much older than me and in some cases dreadfully overweight and says, "She's 24 handicap or she's 28, you could be much better than her." It would be lovely if we could play together occasionally. I know you'll always enjoy your games with your men friends more but it would be nice if we were on holiday – just the two of us – wouldn't it?'

'Yes, it certainly would and it wouldn't be so boring for you when I get home and tell you how I blew a competition by taking a double bogey at the 17th.'

'Yes, that too. I do always try and show an interest but I must confess I don't always know what you are talking about, especially if you have been playing on a course I don't know. Are you ready to eat? I'm afraid it's only cold.'

'Yes, that's fine. I'm quite hungry actually. We only had a snack at El Saler and that is a long time ago.'

They ate their supper in companionable silence and soon after they went to bed, neither having slept very much the previous night, but for rather different reasons. Liz felt relaxed now and went to sleep almost immediately, snuggling up to Tom.

9

Next morning was the usual rush as Tom had his inevitable 8.28 starting time and after he had gone Liz straightened the bed without actually making it – there seemed little point – cleaned her teeth and dabbed a little perfume behind her ears. Make up seemed superfluous, it was not as if Tony had not seen her without it.

There was a tap on the door and Tony walked straight in. Liz had not drawn back the net curtains so that they could not be seen from the road. They ran into each other's arms and kissed passionately.

'I so wanted to ring you last night,' Tony said. 'I presume Tom has told you we're all meeting on the practice ground at 3.30. I would have loved to have been on my own with you but I'm sure the lesson will be more productive this way. Tom seems genuinely interested in the progress you've made and it is a good idea for him to see what I've been teaching you so that he does not undo the good I've done.'

'He could never do that, Tony. I feel twenty years younger than I did a week ago, and that's all down to you. The golf is important, but it's nothing to how I feel.'

'You look great too,' Tony said, 'really glowing and I feel I've come alive again too. It's so sad that you go back to England tomorrow.'

'I think it is probably for the best, don't you? When I think of the risks we've taken, and hopefully got away with. It couldn't last could it?'

'Perhaps you're right but the rest of the week is going to be an awful anti-climax.'

'But you will ring me when you get back won't you and perhaps we can meet sometimes?'

'You bet your sweet life I will, weekdays between eight-thirty and nine – right? I'm back in England at the weekend sometime so I'll ring Monday, or at the latest Tuesday. OK?'

'I'll be waiting by the phone, darling.'

They walked up the stairs to the bedroom with Liz just in front of Tony. He was pulling off her housecoat while she had her hands behind her fumbling with his belt, rather unsuccessfully. When they got upstairs she sat on the bed facing him while she undid his belt and zip and pulled down his trousers while he pulled his tee shirt up over his head.

They made love tenderly, unhurriedly and after they had climaxed and lain together in each other's arms for a while Liz said, 'I want to kiss you all over again, just like the first time.' She gradually worked downwards and by the time she reached his penis it was already lying proudly erect on his stomach, quivering with anticipation. She leant forward to take it in her mouth.

'Do you mind turning round?' Tony said.

Obediently she turned through 180 degrees so that her bottom was against his face and as she took his penis in her hands and placed it in her mouth she could feel his probing tongue parting her lips and finding her clitoris while his semen and her vaginal juices ran down to his mouth and over his chin. They climaxed and Liz turned round and they kissed again, their mouths both tasting of each other.

127

'The taste of each other is fantastic,' Tony said. 'Do you think we should patent it and market it?'

'I wish we could,' Liz replied. 'Even if it didn't sell I'd just love preparing it.'

Tony laughed. 'Me too.' He looked at the clock by the bedside table. 'Christ, is that the time?'

He leapt from the bed and rushed through to the bathroom.

'Which is your toothbrush?' he called.

'The green one.'

Liz could hear him cleaning his teeth. She waited a little while and followed into the bathroom. He was washing his face vigorously now and then he washed his penis carefully pulling back his foreskin and washing its pink tip as well.

'Do you want to remove all traces of me?' Liz asked.

'No, of course not but I must reek of sex and I don't want everyone to know what we've been doing.'

'I suppose not, but is anyone else going to be smelling that part of you?'

'Well, no. They won't obviously. Oh, I don't know. It's probably just habit. Anyway I must dash.'

He dressed hastily, gave her a quick peck and said, 'That was great, see you at 3.30,' and he was gone.

Liz suddenly felt an awful sense of anti-climax. The sex had been wonderful, as good as it had ever been, but . . . perhaps she should not have gone through to the bathroom but the sight of him removing all traces of her so clinically was unnerving, and for the first time she had doubts. Was this just a holiday affair from Tony's point of view, to be forgotten as soon as her plane soared away from San Javier tomorrow? But had she given any impression that she wanted it to be anything more? Yes, she had asked him to phone but equally she had told him that her marriage was important – she had panicked in

Murcia when she found out that the room was not booked in her name. Did she, in fact, want it to be more than a holiday affair? Yes and no. The excitement and the wonderful sex made everything worthwhile when it was happening but if her marriage broke up because of it and she had to leave Oxted and make new friends, leave her Tangent and NADFAS groups where she was a well known and respected figure and, God forbid, the unbearable hassle of a divorce. No, that would all be too much but at the same time if he rang when they got back to England would the excitement of forbidden fruit and the relative boredom of being a suburban housewife mean that she would agree to see him and the affair would restart. It was possible. Tom was away quite a bit for golf competitions and also occasionally on business and as far as she knew Tony was a free agent in Norfolk which wasn't all that far away.

Her feelings at the moment were that she should not let it start up again but she was honest enough to admit to herself that if Tony rang at some time when she was feeling neglected and when Tom had been treating her more like a housekeeper than a wife – then, yes, she would certainly be tempted. And then what about the idea of seeing Tony at La Manga if she went out on her own? The more she thought of that the more dangerous it seemed. The La Manga residents were the biggest scandalmongers she had ever come across, perhaps because of the artificial life they led without the real problems that came with families and jobs. She would only have to be seen having a beer or a golf lesson with Tony and she could think of one or two people who would make it their business to make sure that Tom knew about it. And if Tom knew that Tony was at La Manga at the same time she was. . . . No, that was a definite non-starter, unless Tony lived off the complex

129

that week and they never met except at his hotel. No, she must not think about it.

Tom was in a cheerful mood when he got up to the flat soon after two. He had won his section of the Stableford with 39 points and had won a voucher for three thousand pesetas to be spent at the pro's shop.

'Better think of getting something for you, old girl, if you're going to take the game up. I don't think there is anything I'm needing at the moment.'

'We can't use your prize to buy something for me,' Liz said. 'That would be most unfair.'

'Why not? What's the difference? You can spend the voucher or I can give you the money to buy something. We'll have a look in the pro's shop after your lesson.'

Liz knew the subject was closed. Tom had made his decision and that was it. She had been admiring the Burberry sweaters with the La Manga emblem in the shop and it would be nice to have one of those though they were nearer seven thousand pesetas than three. Perhaps she could make up the difference as she still had some money left from what Tom had given her before the Murcia trip. They walked down to the practice ground and Tony was waiting for them.

'Hi there,' he said. 'How did you do in the competition, Tom? I saw your first drive. It was a beauty.'

'Yes, I got hold of that one, didn't I? In fact I made birdie there – hit a wedge to six feet and finished up with 39 points which was good enough to win. I must say La Manga seemed really easy after El Saler and I played pretty well.'

'Great. Well done. Now then, Liz. Let's see what you've remembered.'

Tony passed her a five iron and she carefully gripped the club the way he had shown her and she had a few practise swings, taking the club back about shoulder high.

'This is what I have been teaching her, Tom – a very short back swing initially but today I'm going to concentrate on the follow through. As she gets more confident she can lengthen her back swing, but, as you know, it's the hitting area which is important in a golf swing and if she has a good follow through, inevitably she will get good weight transference. If she can do all that and keep her head still she'll have a handicap in no time and you can go round picking up all the mixed foursomes prizes. With your ability and a 36 handicap partner you should be a lethal combination.'

Liz started hitting balls with Tony making the odd minor adjustment every now and again and giving plenty of encouragement for all her better shots. Tom was impressed with the regularity with which she made a solid contact with the ball even though he felt she could hit the ball further with a longer back swing. However he could see the sense in Tony's method of teaching as most beginners hit a high percentage of real duff shots and even the occasional complete air shot but Liz was not doing any of that.

'I think you could try a few woods now,' said Tony and teed a ball up for her before passing her a three wood. 'It's just the same swing but you should have the ball a little further forward in your stance. He moved Liz into the correct position.

'She really does keep her head very still which is great. Of course it is always easier on a practice ground without the pressures of a real golf shot where there may be bunkers or ravines to carry but I do hope she will carry on with her golf in England as she has made such a good start. I only have time to show her the basics this trip but I have residential courses in Norfolk in the summer if you would consider that and then we could get on to bunker shots, chipping, putting and everything else.'

'I don't think that will be necessary,' Tom said firmly. 'I can probably help quite a bit and the assistant at my club is very good with beginners.'

'OK,' said Tony not wishing to press the point. 'You will have to watch her alignment – she tends to line up quite a bit left of target but it is a common fault with a beginner. I hope we can have a drink together before you go. I'll probably be in the 37th later on this evening.'

'Yes, perhaps,' Tom said. 'Thanks for your help, anyway. I am impressed with the progress she has made under your expert guidance.'

Liz hit a last few shots, thanked Tony effusively, and she and Tom left the practice ground.

'Do you think he seriously expected me to let you go up to Norfolk on a residential course for chipping, putting and everything else?' Tom spat out the last two words.

'Possibly not but it was nice of him to suggest it and I'm sure there was nothing significant about "everything else". I think his residential courses are very popular and lots of people go. It's not like a private lesson.'

'Hmph! Well you're not bloody going and that's flat. Me pay out money to a bloke who is likely to use it as an excuse to screw my wife, what a bloody joke. I have to say that I am far from happy about what may or may not have gone on at the weekend between you and Tony but I'm not going to ask any more questions. I can't see what it would achieve. If something happened, it happened but I don't want to know that it did. But,' Tom stopped and looked closely at Liz, 'I want you to promise that you won't contact him in England when we get back, because if you do, and I find out, then I really will believe the worst and that could be the end of us.'

'Of course I won't darling,' Liz said taking his arm and smiling up at him.

When they arrived at the Pro's shop Liz went straight

to where the Burberry sweaters were displayed. The pale blue one really appealed to her and they had it in her size. She tried it on and it fitted perfectly.

'What do you think darling?' she asked looking at herself in the mirror.

'I like it, the colour suits you, how much is it?'

'Nearly seven thousand pesetas, I'm afraid. It's too much isn't it?'

'Well it's certainly not cheap. Still never mind. With what I won last week I've got six thousand in vouchers so it's only another fiver. We'll take it,' he said to the pretty Spanish girl who was hovering around.

'You are good to me Tom. I could pay the difference as I've still got some money left from Murcia.' Liz put her arm round Tom and snuggled up to him.

'No, don't worry. I'll do the lot. Just make sure I don't have cause to regret it.'

He paid for the sweater and they made their way to the car.

'What's happening this evening?' Liz asked.

'Oh, didn't I say? Sorry. The gang are coming to us for a drink at about seven and then we are all going down to the Village for a meal. We've got a table.'

'That's super. I hoped we'd all do something together on our last night.'

Liz was relieved that they were going out. She had not fancied an evening with Tom alone in case he changed his mind about asking questions. She could not have faced that and it was always so much more difficult to remember lies than the truth – she would have been bound to contradict herself at some stage.

They went back to the flat and read for a while before Liz went up to change and shower and then got out the last of their crisps, olives and nuts ready for the arrival of their friends. At five to seven Tom went up and changed his shirt but that, he felt was sufficient for a meal with friends at the Village, which was quite a small restaurant only seating thirty or forty people. It was at Los Belones only a mile or so from the complex and was owned and run by an English woman universally known as Jill, and it seemed questionable if anyone knew her surname. A few people who had been coming to La Manga for a while referred to her as Young Jill as her mother and father used to have a rather larger restaurant on the road to El Algar but had sold that about eighteen months previously. Young Jill did similar food which meant that many of her parent's old customers came to her. The food in some ways was rather anglicised but there were a few genuinely Spanish dishes and also a couple of oriental ones. All visible staff were female and attractive so that a very high proportion of golfers who had come out for a stag holiday went there virtually every night, and English was spoken almost without exception. Very few Spanish people ever went to the restaurant but there was always a good atmosphere and sometimes a singsong developed towards the end of the evening. Tom probably enjoyed it more than Liz who always liked to struggle with a Spanish menu and was quite prepared to put up with the odd rather unexpected dish when her translation had gone awry. She also liked to eat genuinely Spanish dishes like rabbit with garlic which was something she had never come across in England. The pork also, was very different in Spain as Spaniards do not like crackling or fat so that pork dishes are made entirely from lean meat and are often served as steaks. Traditional roast pork would only be found in an English-owned restaurant. Liz also enjoyed the *cocidos* or stews which could contain almost anything, but normally had a vegetable base mixed with anything else which happened to be handy at the time.

They had a pleasant evening together though it was

noticeable that Gilbert was much nicer to everyone else than he was to Jane. Liz was eager to have a private word with Jane to find out what the problem was. She did not have long to wait before Jane got up to go to the loo and Liz quickly followed her. When she got to the cloakroom Jane was standing at one of the basins putting on some fresh lipstick. Liz tried the door of the loo, which swung open.

'Good, we are on our own. What ever has got into Gilbert? He's being foul to you.'

'Thank God you're here Liz. I've got to talk to someone. To use his words: "He's deeply suspicious about what went on last weekend but he's not going to question me about it. He does not know what that would achieve," but he's made me promise I won't see James again.'

'Gosh, really! That's more or less exactly what Tom said to me about Tony. They must have discussed it together and decided that's the best course of action.'

'Sounds bloody like it doesn't it? Still it's pretty sensible don't you think? What would a cross-examination achieve? If we are extra nice when we get home it will blow over in no time. It's a lot of nonsense really.'

They both heard someone go into the gents next door. Liz held her finger to her lips.

'I really enjoyed my Nasi Goreng. I do stir fries at home but I can never buy prawns as nice as the ones here.'

'No, it seems impossible doesn't it? These ones are so plump and full of flavour. I asked Jill where she got them but she never discloses where she buys anything.'

'No, she won't, will she, still I suppose it is understandable, if we all went there to buy, the quality would probably drop off and even worse for Jill we'd probably cook more at home instead of coming here. Stir fries are jolly easy to do, even on a two-ring hob.'

135

They came out of the ladies together, almost colliding with Gilbert who was coming out of the gents.

'What a jolly domestic little conversation,' he said bitterly. 'I thought you might have something more interesting to talk about.'

'I don't know what that is supposed to mean,' replied Jane. 'Liz and I talk about food quite a lot.'

'And what may I ask is or was "a lot of nonsense" '?

'Oh weren't you having a nice old rubberneck! If you must know Liz and I think it's a lot of nonsense the amount we spend eating out when we could quite easily take it in turns to prepare a meal at our flats, at least some of the evenings. Satisfied?'

'Not really but I guess it will have to do. Do you two want another coffee or shall we move on?'

'Don't mind at all, whatever everyone else wants to do. Are we going to the 37th?' Liz asked.

'I don't think so. Tom doesn't seem very keen and he says that Brian Chapman's new piano bar at La Quinta opens tonight so we could give that a whirl.'

'Oh yes, do let's,' said Jane. 'It would be nice to go somewhere different.'

Liz was disappointed not to be going to the 37th and seeing Tony, but also slightly relieved as she felt it would take very little to get Tom going again and he had been fine all evening – in fact ever since their little chat on the way back from the practice ground without a mention of Tony or his suspicions. There was a lively atmosphere at the piano bar which had been renamed 'Chapmas Marquee' and had been decorated rather like the inside of a tent. Brian was singing no end of request numbers with his voice which was unusually strong for such a small man. They all danced a bit but it was noticeable that Gilbert danced with everyone except Jane who was beginning to drink heavily and was getting more and more tight, beginning to slur her words and when Tom danced with her she made several false steps and he had to hold her tightly to save her from falling.

'I think what we all need is some black coffee,' Tom said tactfully when they returned to the table.

'I don' wanna bloody coffee,' Jane said, 'I wanna brandy, Carlos Primero.'

Gilbert rose to his feet.

'You're not having anything more to drink, Jane,' he said firmly. 'I'm taking you home right now.' And he led her protesting out of the room.

'She's in a bad way,' Tom said. 'Would anyone like another drink or a coffee or shall we all make a move?'

'I'm quite happy to go,' Liz said. 'I've enjoyed it here but I don't want to be too late. I hate arriving in England feeling dead beat.'

There were murmurs of assent and cries of 'See you at the airport, if not before,' before they all made their way back to their respective apartments.

'Jane was really drunk,' Tom said, 'not a pretty sight. Does she often get like that?'

'Not to my knowledge,' Liz replied, 'but I must say she has been drinking quite a lot this holiday and Gilbert was being really nasty to her this evening, wasn't he?'

'Mm, I suppose he was but I can't say I'm surprised. I think I'd be much the same if I thought you'd been carrying on with that drip, James. At least I can see that Tony is an attractive man and quite a likeable bloke. I'd probably thoroughly enjoy his company if you weren't around.'

'Well he's not around now, is he?' said Liz slipping her arm through Tom's as they walked down to the flat from the car park. They undressed quickly and went to bed and although they did not make love they kissed each other tenderly goodnight and were soon fast asleep.

10

Next morning Tom got up first and made coffee, bringing it to Liz in bed with a peeled pear and orange which they shared. Liz could not help wondering what might have been done with the fruit if Tony had brought it, but this was comfortable and companionable with no worries or anxieties. This was really what middle age was about she thought.

'What are your plans for today Tom? Are you going to have a last game of golf?'

'No, I don't think so. I've nothing arranged so I thought I'd give you a hand cleaning this place up and packing and then perhaps we could go down to Cabo and have a Spanish lunch at La Tana. You always say you never have a proper lunch in Spain and I doubt if the food on the plane will be up to much.'

'Oh, that sounds lovely – you are good to me.'

So it happened that they spent the whole day together – the first and only such day of their holiday – and Tony's name was never mentioned by either of them. Liz would have liked to have seen him or even spoken on the phone, just to say goodbye but she did not want to rock the boat and Tom was being helpful and attentive. They had their lunch on the terrace at La Tana relishing the warm sunshine and conscious of the fact that it would be some time before they would eat out of doors again.

As a main course they had sea bass baked in salt and Liz was fascinated by the number of Spaniards having lunch at the restaurant with hardly an English word being spoken. She thought there was much to be said for the siesta system, enabling one to enjoy a good lunch as opposed to the quick sandwich and pint of beer which Tom usually had in England. By the time they got back from lunch there was only time to put their cases in the car, leave the keys of the apartment at the hotel and make their way to the airport at San Javier.

The others were already there when they arrived, all looking very different in relatively formal clothes with the men wearing ties with their jackets slung over their arms and the women in sweaters and skirts, carrying raincoats. Some of the travellers were still dressed Spanish-style in tee shirts and shorts, but Liz and Tom had done the trip often enough to know how it felt arriving at Gatwick in February at about nine thirty in the evening, dressed like that. Gilbert looked tired and Jane was wearing dark glasses and rather too much make-up. Everyone seemed rather subdued and Liz was interested to see that Jane was drinking coffee instead of the usual gin and tonic. Liz noticed that James was on the same flight but he was over in the far corner and Jane made no effort to speak to him or him to her.

They were told that the plane was on time and sure enough it landed only half an hour or so after they arrived so with the quick turn round they would be on their way in another half hour or so. Tom went out of the reception area to see the passengers disembark but apparently there were no great buddies of his on the flight though inevitably there were a few people whom he had met playing golf on previous holidays and a number of people who worked on the complex.

139

All eight promised to keep in touch when they got home but Liz wondered if it would be any different this year. They always promised to do so but usually nothing happened until about October when one of the men would ring round to check if everyone was going out again and if so what seemed suitable dates. Liz certainly thought she would contact Jane because she was worried about her relationship with Gilbert and, of course, they did share a secret. She didn't live very far away and it would be nice to meet for lunch and find out if she and Gilbert had got their act together again and if she was still seeing James. Jane, in turn, would want to know if she had heard from Tony and whether or not they had met or planned to do so. Yes, she would definitely ring Jane in a week or two and fix something up. The flight back was uneventful and as luck would have it Tom and Liz's cases were some of the first to come on to the carousel so that they got home soon after eleven. Liz was very touched when they got inside as all the post had been picked up and put on the dining table together with a vase of flowers and a note from Jean saying, 'Welcome Home Ma and Pa'.

'Isn't she sweet?' Liz said. 'She must have driven down from London specially.'

'Yes, she's a good kid,' Tom agreed. 'I just hope she will be happy with Chris. He seems all right but so many marriages break up in no time nowadays.'

'Well, if she does as well as us, she won't do badly, will she?'

'No, I guess not. I hope you will work at your golf now you're back. You need an interest. You're too pretty to be a bored housewife and with the kids off your hands I don't think you really have enough to occupy yourself. NADFAS and Tangent don't exactly stretch you.'

'Oh, I will, I will. I was thinking on the plane who I knew who I could ask if they would put up with me. I'm longing to try a proper round but I appreciate that I'll have to spend some time on a driving range first. Margaret Deeble has only just started and I think she has just become a member of West Kent so she may be able to help. Oh, and there is Pat Cowan as well, I'm not sure how good she is, but I think she plays at Tandridge.'

'Great. I'll see what I can arrange through my golfing friends. I'm sure some of them must have wives who have only just started. You see what happens is that you must play some rounds with women who are members of a club and have an official handicap, and they can mark a card for you. When you have done three scores which are not more than 45 over the standard scratch score of the course we can start making enquiries about getting you into a club, but I don't think there is one round here that would consider an application from a total beginner. Kingswood is probably going to be the best bet because preference is always given to the wife of an existing member.'

'That would be super, but I'm sure it is going to take some time before I can manage the required scores.'

'I don't know. You hit the ball pretty well at La Manga and I intend to help you as much as I can. I'm very conscious that I neglected you this holiday and I'm not going to do that again. We've spent a nice day together today and next time we go to Spain I promise I'm going to spend much more time with you – and we'll play some golf together,' Tom added as an after-thought.

Liz laughed. 'Don't go too far, Tom. It's a lovely idea but you enjoy your golf with the chaps so much. I don't think playing me for money would ever have quite the same appeal as taking a few pounds from your regular cronies.'

'Well, I'm not suggesting that I would play all my golf with you but there are lots of days when we could have nine holes together in the late afternoon or early evening and when you get a handicap we could play in the four ball together on Fridays.'

Again Liz laughed. 'Take it easy Tom. I may never get a handicap. I'm sure it is completely different all on your own on a golf course with bunkers and lakes and streams and things. Not a bit like a practice ground with a good teacher standing beside you. Let's just take it stage by stage. Are you going to open the post tonight, and if so would you like a nightcap?'

'Yes to both questions. I'll have a Spanish brandy please. I'll just see if there is anything urgent in the post and if there is I'll take it to the office tomorrow and sort it out from there.'

'I thought you'd say that. I'll leave you to it then and do some unpacking,' Liz said, bringing him a healthy Ciento y Tres brandy. 'I'll just take a little Melocoton upstairs with me.'

An hour or so later Tom came upstairs and Liz was already in bed reading her book.

'Nothing too drastic, I'm glad to say. We've got a red phone bill. I don't know what happened to the first one and they have asked me to play in the Hewitt again. I just hope I can play as well as I did most of the time in Spain. There is also a slight possibility of a trip to Malaysia in the autumn with the Seniors. I'd love to be selected for that, never having been to that part of the world and wives can come too, which would make it better still.'

'Mm, that does sound lovely – that really would be something to look forward to. When will you know if you are selected?'

'I don't know love. At the moment they are just asking if I would like to be considered, so I expect quite a lot of people have been asked that question. A couple of months or so probably. Soon Tom was in bed also and cuddled up to Liz, but made no move to make love. Liz roused him

142

with her hand and they made love, lying on their sides and kissing each other tenderly. When they had finished Tom said, 'Don't ever leave me Liz, I love you so much, I couldn't bear a life without you.'

'I won't leave you, Tom. Today has been perfect and when you retire we can have lots and lots of days together, just like today.'

'Yes, I hope so but there is another couple of years to go before I can retire. Let's work hard to make those few years good too.'

'Yes, darling, we can do it,' Liz replied snuggling up to Tom.

Life went back to normal with Tom getting home quite late as he had a lot of work to catch up with at his office, and Liz performed her usual housewifely duties.

On Friday morning the phone rang at about nine o'clock and Liz answered, 'Oxted 32157.'

'Hi, Liz. It's me, Jane.'

'Jane. How nice to hear from you. How are you?'

'Bloody awful, thanks – look, I don't want to talk on the phone but could you meet me for lunch? I must talk to someone or I'll go mad and you are really the only one.'

'Yes, of course. Where do you suggest and when?'

'Do you know that pub at Wotton just this side of Dorking on the Guildford road?'

'Oh yes. I know it very well. Tom always raves about the beer there so we sometimes go there for a drink and I drive back.'

'That's great. Could you be there at about twelve-thirty?'

'Yes, sure. No problem. I'll see you there and we can have a good old chin wag.'

'Thanks Liz. I feel better already. 'Bye.'

Liz put the phone down. Obviously things were still not good between Jane and Gilbert. I wonder why, she mused

143

when Tom seems to have recovered his equanimity completely and in fact was being more solicitous and attentive than he had been for ages. He'd even bought her some flowers the day before, and roses too – in February.

When Liz arrived at Wotton, Jane was already there and was well outside a gin and tonic.

'Thank God you've come,' Jane said, 'what are you going to have to drink?'

'I'd like a dry spritzer please,' Liz replied.

Jane went up to the bar and came back with the spritzer and another gin and tonic for herself.

'Don't you think you should go easy on the gin, Jane, you are driving remember and you don't want to lose your licence.'

'Bugger my bloody licence. Gin is the only thing keeping me sane at the moment.'

'Tell me all about it then. What's the trouble?'

'Well, you know Gilbert said he wasn't going to ask any questions about last weekend. Well, he didn't, in Spain. He just didn't speak to me at all out there which was more or less OK – a bit miserable, but OK – but when we were waiting for our cases at Gatwick who should come wandering over but dear old James. He said he had just come over to say goodbye and how much he had enjoyed our tennis at La Manga and perhaps I'd come over and have a game with him at Maidenhead sometime. I started to make some sort of non-committal answer but that did it. Gilbert went mad and tried to hit James, apart from shouting and screaming like a madman. I managed to restrain him but ever since it's been a sort of third degree, all the way back from Gatwick in the car and more or less every waking hour since. Apparently when he got back from El Saler he wandered down to the tennis club and pretended to be a bloody tree or something. Anyway he saw James and me come off court and apparently James

144

put his arm round me and we kissed. It can't have been more than a blinking peck I'm sure but Gilbert seems totally convinced that it was proof of infidelity and I don't think he is going to rest unless and until I've admitted it.'

'God, how awful. Does he think James came to Murcia?'

'No, I don't think so. My little story about the Spanish waiter seems to have been pretty convincing and he thinks highly of you and obviously you would not have connived at some extra marital affair, so aren't you the lucky one? No, he definitely suspects the infidelity took place at La Manga, but I think the real trouble is that James is absolutely the type of man he least admires, you know, affected voice, not much chin, long hair, bit over-weight, flashy clothes.'

'Yes, I see what you mean. I've been quite lucky in that way because Tom quite admires Tony and sees him as a definite threat. He said so himself. He recognizes Tony as a man who is very attractive to women and he has been wonderful to me ever since we got back. He even bought me roses yesterday.'

'Christ. The only flowers Gilbert would buy me would be lilies for my grave, I should think. Are you ready for another drink?'

'No, I'm fine thanks and Jane, please don't have another one. Let's order some food and perhaps we'll have a glass of wine with that.'

'You please yourself but I'm having another gin.'

Jane got up and bought another gin and tonic, Liz noticing that this one, at least, was a double. Liz wondered if she should offer to drive Jane home. It wasn't just Jane and her licence but if there were an accident innocent people could be injured or even killed.

'You're always very sane and level-headed, Liz. What do you reckon I should do?' Jane asked when she came back with her drink. 'I don't know how long I can hold out like this. I'm just glad you don't seem to be involved as well and that Tom is behaving nicely to you. Come on. What do you suggest?'

'Well first of all do you still love Gilbert? Do you want to stay married to him?'

'I think love is probably a bit strong, but certainly if we can get our relationship back on an even keel I have no wish for our marriage to end. I like to have the odd fling but Gilbert and I get on all right – or used to. We like our house, we've got lots of mutual friends and I suppose quite a few separate ones, he through work and golf and me mostly through tennis but we always said that was good and that we had more to talk to each other about because of it.'

'Mm. What about your sex life? Do you often make love?'

'Infrequently, I suppose. That's one word, not two,' Jane said smiling. 'Well, I suppose about once a week on average, but since last weekend he has not come near me. I mean we share a bed but he's on one side and I'm on the other. There's a hell of a gap in the middle.'

'And when you do make love, who initiates it?' Liz continued.

'Oh, always Gilbert. I suppose I sometimes try and look sexy or may make a provocative remark but never more than that. I think it all started from very early in our marriage when I started fondling his willie and was told very firmly not to act like a tart. Thinking about it maybe that's why I enjoy the odd bit of extra-marital sex. I like rousing a man. It gives one a sense of power, don't you think?'

'Yes, I love it but it's a shame if you can't do this with Gilbert because somehow I think you've got to show him that you want him and find him desirable, and then you

146

must make love. A man who has just had a good screw is so much more amenable, his bitterness seems to drain away with his semen.'

'You're probably right, Liz. I'm sorry to put you in the role of an agony aunt, but you're jolly good at it. I'll have to think how I can turn Gilbert on. Let's go and get something to eat.'

Liz ordered a lasagne and Jane a canneloni and they each ordered a glass of red wine.

'Has James contacted you since you got back?' Liz asked as they sat down with their food.

'Oh yes. Good old James. He rang yesterday, fortunately when Gilbert was out, suggesting we met up at the weekend. I told him there was no chance and not to ring again. Don't call me, I'll call you, I said.'

'He seems pretty keen I must say. How keen are you?'

'Not at all really. He was fine at La Manga but I don't think I want to see him back here, certainly not in present circumstances. What about Tony? Has he been on the blower?'

'No, not yet. Anyway he's not back from Spain until tomorrow or Sunday, because, of course, he is driving back. In many ways I hope he doesn't ring because I have to say my feelings for him frighten me a bit. It's a sort of overpowering lust which just plays havoc with my morals and common sense. I really don't want to risk my marriage, and with Tom behaving as he has these last few days I feel our marriage is really great.'

'Lucky you. Thanks for coming over, Liz. It's helped me a lot just to talk about it. I feel much more relaxed now. I can probably get back to Guildford without another gin. I was so strung up before you came.'

'There's no rush,' Liz said, 'let's have a coffee first. I'm still worried about you driving. Were those all double gins you had?'

'No, only two of them. Honestly I'm fine now. I ate loads of canneloni. I'll be OK. I've got to get back and rehearse my Mata Hari number. D'you think I could do the dance of the seven veils?'

They were both laughing as they walked out of the pub.

'You could try,' Liz said, 'but you know Gilbert best. Why don't you get him a drink when he comes home and give him his favourite supper by the fire? Touch him tenderly when you walk by. I'm sure that sort of thing would help.'

'Yeah, I guess so. I'll see what I can think of in the car, and maybe buy some salmon on the way back. He always likes that. Thanks again for coming over, Liz. You've been a great help. I'll give you a ring early next week and let you know how I get on.'

Jane got into her red Astra GTE and accelerated fast down the drive towards the A25. Liz got into her Peugeot 205 and drove at a much more sedate pace before turning right towards Dorking. She hoped Jane would be all right. She had to be over the limit. She wondered if she should tell Tom about their lunch together. Yes, why not? They were friends weren't they? Why shouldn't they meet for lunch?

Tom got back from work just after seven, as usual, and the phone started to ring as he came through the front door. He picked it up.

'Hello, Tom Waldren speaking.' . . . 'Gilbert. How are you old son? Bloody awful being back at work isn't it?' . . . 'Oh, God, really. Christ, I am sorry. Is there anything I can do?' . . . 'You want to speak to Liz. Yes, of course. I'll give her a shout. Hold on.'

Tom put his hand over the mouthpiece. 'Liz,' his voice boomed throughout the house and Liz came rushing through from the kitchen where she had been preparing supper.

148

'It's Gilbert – apparently Jane has been done for driving over the limit and she is banged up in Guildford police station. He wants to speak to you.'

'Yes, yes of course,' Liz said taking the phone from Tom.

'Hello Gilbert' . . . 'Yes, Tom has just told me. How awful. I am sorry. There wasn't an accident was there?' . . . 'Oh, thank goodness for that.' . . . 'Yes, yes we did at Wotton.' . . . 'Well, yes she did have two or three gins. I wanted her to have some coffee but she insisted she was all right. If only she had listened to me and not been in such a hurry.' . . . 'Yes, she suggested this morning that we meet for lunch.' . . . 'She's worried about your relationship, Gilbert. She was ever so unhappy but she did seem a bit better when she left me. Was she much over the limit?' . . . 'Sixty-five. That's quite a bit over isn't it?' . . . 'Yes, I suppose so. Well give her our love and tell her I'll ring her in the morning.' . . . 'Yes. OK, bye.' Liz put the phone down and put an arm round Tom.

'I didn't hear you come in. I suppose it was the television. Isn't that awful and I feel partly responsible having been with her at lunch time although I did discourage her from drinking and suggested we had a coffee before we left. What happened was that Jane rang this morning – she sounded in an awful state and asked if I could meet her for lunch at that pub in Wotton where you like the beer so much. Well, of course I said "Yes" and she did have at least three gins and a glass of wine.'

'All of that I should think if she was sixty-five,' Tom said. 'Still never mind – go on.'

'Well, apparently Gilbert is giving her a really hard time about James – you know, the chap she played tennis with – and it's really getting Jane down, well, she just wanted a chat really.'

'Mm, can't say I'm surprised. He talked to me about it

149

at La Manga. He really took a dislike to that bloke and he saw them kissing at the tennis club the day we got back from El Saler. I said the best thing was to try and forget it and I thought I'd convinced him, but obviously something got him going again.'

'Oh yes. I think I know what that was. Apparently James came up to them when they were waiting for their cases at Gatwick and suggested that Jane should come over to Maidenhead for a game of tennis. Well, you know how mild Gilbert usually is but apparently he just flew off the handle. He said something like "Piss off you bloody ponce. Neither my wife nor I ever want to see you or speak to you again," and then went to throw a punch at James. James tried to stammer some sort of explanation but Jane had to restrain Gilbert and ever since she has been having a sort of third-degree inquisition. How often had they played tennis? Who had they played with? What else had they done together? Had James ever been to their flat? Had she ever been to James' place etc, etc and Jane isn't keen on James anyway. I'm not saying she didn't enjoy his company at La Manga and their tennis but she told me at lunch she didn't want to see him again.'

'Did she indeed? I think it would be good if you tell Gilbert that. I wonder if you can still catch him. He was just on his way to Guildford police station to pick her up.'

'I'll certainly try. It might reassure him, mightn't it?'

Liz looked up their number and dialled but there was no reply.

'No reply,' she said. 'Still, I'll mention it when I ring tomorrow. Another of their problems is that they don't have much of a sex life but I don't see how I can help in that respect. A nice love really is the best way to make up, isn't it darling?'

'Certainly is,' Tom replied putting his arm round Liz and kissing her on the forehead.

After supper they watched television with Tom reading the paper simultaneously and were just thinking of going to bed when the telephone rang.

'Hello, Tom Waldren speaking.' . . . 'Gilbert – are you all right old chap?' . . . 'Oh my God! I can't believe it.' . . . 'The police are coming round you say. How on earth did it happen?' . . . 'Well you've just got to tell them the truth exactly as you've told me. Obviously it was an accident. I'm sure they are not going to suggest anything else.' . . . 'They're there now?' . . . 'OK. I'll call you in the morning.' . . . 'Yes. Bye.' Tom put the phone down slowly and turned to Liz who was watching him anxiously.

'It's Jane isn't it? What's happened, Tom?'

Tom put his arms round her. 'She's dead, Liz.'

'Dead? Dead? How?'

'I don't know if I've got the whole story but as I understand it Gilbert went to Guildford police station straight after speaking to us to bring her home and apparently the form filling and things took ages and from what I can gather Gilbert was lecturing her on the way back about her drinking and Jane was crying and upset. Then the first thing she did when she got home was pour herself a bloody great brandy, Gilbert saw red and hit her and she fell with her head striking one of those big firedogs they have and she died instantly. Gilbert tried giving her the kiss of life but that didn't work so he called an ambulance. When they came they confirmed that she was dead and said they would have to call in the police and they arrived just as we finished our conversation.'

'What a terrible thing to happen. If only I had told Gilbert about Jane not wanting to see James again, perhaps it would have made all the difference. I feel awful. I've got to be partly to blame. And letting her drive home after lunch as well.'

'I don't know what more you could have done. From

what you've told me you acted very responsibly. Don't blame yourself, love. It's just a tragic accident.'

Liz had an awful sinking feeling in her stomach and felt slightly sick. How much would the police investigate? she wondered. Would they be concerned about the cause of Gilbert and Jane's rows?

'I just can't understand Gilbert hitting Jane. It seems so out of character. But then he nearly hit James at Gatwick. You just can't judge by appearances, can you? Even when you know someone well. Is there anything we can do?'

'I don't think so, luv. I said I'd ring in the morning and obviously we'll go to the funeral but I really can't think what we could do to help. We could ask Gilbert over for supper or something but he's got his family and I imagine he'll want to be with them.'

They went to bed but neither of them slept well with Jane's death uppermost in their minds and Liz worried as to the extent of the police investigation and whether the story of her relationship with Tony would come out. She wished she could talk to Tony but he wasn't back from La Manga yet and she couldn't ring him at Sheringham until Monday when Tom had gone to work. Well, possibly she could try sometime on Sunday if Tom went off to golf, but he hadn't said anything about playing. She felt rather like Jane had on Friday, that it would be nice to talk to someone who knew the whole story.

11

Tom rang Gilbert's number at about nine next morning but without response.

'No reply, old girl. I'll leave it until just before lunch and if there is still no reply I think I'll ring Guildford police. Is there anything you want me to do or shall I get on with a bit of gardening. It's amazing how untidy everything is after only a fortnight away.'

'No, I don't think so, thank you Tom. I'll have to go down to the shops and get some food for tomorrow sometime, but I don't need you for that. What sort of joint would you like?'

'Oh beef, I think. I always hanker after roast beef after a week or two in Spain.'

Tom went out to the garden and Liz put the breakfast things in the dishwasher, made the bed, tidied up the house a bit and was just about to leave the house to do the shopping when the phone rang. She picked it up.

'Oxted 32157.'

'Mrs Waldren?' an unfamiliar voice said.

'Yes, this is Liz Waldren speaking. Who is that?'

'This is Guildford police. Detective Inspector Hoskings speaking, I think you know that Mrs Kennedy is dead.'

'Yes, Gilbert telephoned last night. Isn't it awful?'

'Yes, madam. We have a full statement from Mr

153

Kennedy, of course, but I understand you had lunch with Mrs Kennedy yesterday. Is that so?'

'Yes, yes I did.'

'We wondered, Mrs Waldren, if you would come to the station and give us a statement. It would help us in getting a full picture of the events leading up to Mrs Kennedy's death. Could you come to Guildford police station this afternoon? Would that be possible?'

'Yes, yes of course. At what time?'

'Would about two o'clock be convenient madam?'

'Yes, that would be fine.'

'Thank you madam. If you ask the desk sergeant for me, Detective Inspector Hoskings, he will bring you straight to my office. Goodbye Mrs Waldren.'

'Y-yes. Goodbye Inspector.'

The line went dead and Liz shivered. What was she going to say? What had Gilbert said? He had made a full statement, but what did that mean? What had Gilbert and Jane rowed about? The drinking or the suspected infidelity or both? She must keep Tony's name out of it whatever happened. Would there be a court case? Would she have to give evidence? There could well be a manslaughter charge or even – she shivered again – murder. That would mean a trial and she could well be called to give evidence. If Jane's infidelity came out then almost certainly hers would also and then what would happen? She must tell Tom that she had to go to Guildford police station. She couldn't hide that from him. She went out to the garden.

'Darling,' she called.

Tom's head appeared above a shrub which had been partially blown over during the gales while they were away.

'Yes, what is it?'

'Are you playing golf this afternoon?'

'Yes, probably. I can finish this off tomorrow if necessary. I'll probably go up about one. Why?'

'It's just that Guildford police have been on the phone. They want me to go over there this afternoon and make a statement. I've got to be there at two.'

'I'll take you. Bugger the golf. I hadn't arranged anything anyway.'

Liz felt uneasy. 'No, Tom. You carry on as usual. I'll be fine. You know how much you enjoy your Saturday golf and you haven't seen your chums at Kingswood for three weeks now.'

'Certainly not. I wouldn't think of it. It's bound to be a bit traumatic for you. I'm taking you and that is final. You go and do your bits of shopping and we'll leave when you get back. We'll have a pub lunch on the way.'

Liz knew it was no good arguing. 'Well, if you are sure. Just as long as we don't go to the pub at Wotton. I couldn't face that.'

'No, of course not. There are plenty of other places. We'll leave soon after twelve.'

Liz went down to the shops and bought a nice rib of beef and some vegetables and was appalled at the price she was paying for the latter compared with Spain. She also bought some cheese and fruit. At least there is a better selection of cheese she thought and a little bit cheaper too but the fruit seemed very dear.

She was back at the house at about twelve and by ten past they were on their way to Guildford in Tom's Rover Vitesse. They stopped at a pub just outside Leatherhead and both had ploughmans, Tom having a pint of bitter and Liz a tomato juice. She didn't think she should have anything alcoholic before being interviewed by the police and Tom must have been conscious of the fact that he was going to a police station as he only had the one pint. They got to Guildford police station just before two and they

155

walked up to the desk together. A rather overweight sergeant came up to them.

'Can I help you?' he said.

'My name is Liz Waldren. I have an appointment with Inspector Hoskings.'

'Yes madam, we are expecting you. And who are you, sir?' he added turning to Tom.

'I'm Tom Waldren. This lady's husband.'

'Thank you sir. I'll tell the Inspector you are here.' He picked up the phone and dialled a number.

'Mrs Waldren is here to see you, sir and her husband is here as well.' There was a pause.

'Yes, sir. Right away sir.' He put the phone down. 'The Inspector would like to see you too, sir,' the sergeant said to Tom.

'Do you mind waiting, Madam. If you would take a seat over there madam, and if you would follow the constable, sir. Jones, will you take this gentleman to Inspector Hoskings' office.'

A young fair-haired policeman, who looked about seventeen got up from behind a desk.

'If you would follow me, sir.'

'Yes, yes of course. I didn't know the Inspector would want to see me. I just brought my wife along.'

'I'm sure the Inspector will explain, sir.'

Tom followed the young policeman along a passage, up some stairs, along another passage and the constable knocked on a door. It was opened by a small well-dressed man in his mid-thirties.

'Mr Waldren – good of you to see me. Thank you constable. Come in Mr Waldren.'

Tom entered a spacious but sparsely furnished office and another man in his mid-twenties rose to his feet.

'This is Detective Sergeant Parsons. He will make notes of what we say and we may ask you to make a statement later. It's just background information we need, but this is a nasty business and we need as much background as we can get.'

'I know it is a nasty business, Inspector, but surely it was just a tragic accident.'

'That is what we have to find out, sir. As far as we know there were no witnesses but the fact is that Mrs Kennedy is dead, so on the face of it Mr Kennedy could be charged with manslaughter or even murder.'

'Oh my God, I was just thinking of accidental death, well anything I can do to help, Inspector.'

'First of all Mr Waldren, can I say that I don't want you making conclusions or guesses. I just want you to answer my questions truthfully and if you don't know the answer don't be afraid to say so. You are not being charged with anything so you have nothing to fear. Is that clear?'

'Yes, of course. What do you want to know Inspector?'

First they took Tom's name, age, address and occupation.

'How long have you known Mr Kennedy?'

'About five years.'

'Did you know him well?'

'Quite well, but mainly from holidays in Spain. We only used to meet two or three times a year over here and that was normally to play golf. He would come over to Kingswood and I would go to Worplesdon. We often talked about meeting for dinner with our wives but it only came off once when we went over to their place.'

'How long have you known Mrs Kennedy?'

'Three years almost exactly. I met her the first time she and Gilbert came to La Manga with us.'

'What sort of person was she?'

'I didn't know her very well but she was attractive, vivacious, good fun, very keen on tennis. She didn't play golf.'

157

'Did she drink a lot?'

'Well, I never thought so until this holiday but yes – she did drink a lot this holiday – mainly gin.'

'Did you ever see her drunk?'

'Not really drunk, not in a sense of being incapable but sometimes she would slur her words a bit and perhaps stagger a little at the end of an evening but then I guess we all drink a bit more than usual on holiday. I know I do.'

'Did you ever hear Mr Kennedy censure her about her drinking?'

'No, but I know he was worried about it. He told me so and he would sometimes say, "Haven't you had enough, Jane?" '

'Do you know a Mr James Hislop?'

'Not really. I met him for about five minutes when he came to our flat for a drink but I didn't really speak to him.'

'He came to your flat for a drink? Was he with Mrs Kennedy?'

'Yes.'

'Was Mr Kennedy there as well?'

'No.'

'Did that strike you as strange?'

'No, not really. Gilbert and I had been away playing golf and we got back earlier than expected. My wife had asked them up for a drink and when Jane found out we were back they left almost immediately.'

'Were Mrs Kennedy and Mr Hislop having an affair?'

'I don't know.'

'Do you think they were having an affair?'

'Again, I don't know. I know Gilbert suspected it. He had seen them kissing. I said that at worst it was just a holiday affair and that he should ignore it as I was doing with my wife.'

'Was your wife having an affair?'

158

'I don't know. I hope not but there was a golf pro down there – a notorious womaniser – who was paying her a lot of attention.'

'But you ignored this?'

'Well, not exactly but I love my wife, Inspector, and I think she loves me. I would hate our marriage to break up and I don't think an inquisition would help anything. I neglected my wife on this holiday, as Gilbert neglected Jane, looking back on it, and I'm not going to make the same mistake again.'

'Did you see Mr and Mrs Kennedy and Mr Hislop at Gatwick?'

'No, but our luggage came off the plane very quickly. I think there was some kind of altercation after we left.'

'Why do you say that?'

'My wife told me. Jane said something to her about it at lunch yesterday.'

'What else did your wife tell you about lunch yesterday?'

'I think you should ask her that question.'

'But I am asking you Mr Waldren. Remember Mr Kennedy could face a charge of murder and your wife might not say the same to me as she did to you. You are her husband and know the people involved. Please remember Mr Waldren, neither you nor your wife are facing any charges. Now, I ask you again, what did your wife tell you about lunch yesterday?'

'Well, not a lot really. She mentioned this Gatwick business. Apparently Hislop had come over and suggested Jane should come over for a game of tennis at Maidenhead and Gilbert blew his top and said that neither he nor Jane ever wanted to see him again and Gilbert went to throw a punch at Hislop but Jane restrained him and ever since he had been giving Jane a sort of third degree about Hislop. How often had they

159

met? Had he been to their flat? Had she been to his, etc and it was getting her down so she asked Liz to meet her for lunch so they could have a chat. That's about all I know really.'

'Would you say Mr Kennedy is a violent man?'

'No, not at all. Quite the reverse in fact. I was amazed to hear about the Gatwick business. I think it must have been because he had taken a violent dislike to Hislop and was worried about his relationship with Jane.'

'Does it surprise you that Mr Kennedy says he struck his wife?'

'Yes, very much but he told me he did. Jealousy is a very strong emotion.'

'Mr Kennedy told you he had struck his wife? When was that?'

'Last night. He rang just after it had happened. Immediately before the police arrived at his house.'

'What exactly did Mr Kennedy say to you?'

'I don't remember the exact words – he was very upset obviously but he said he had harangued her about her drinking in the car on the way back from here and then when they got home the first thing she did was to pour herself a large brandy. He blew his top and hit her. She fell and caught her head on one of their cast iron fire dogs. He tried the kiss of life unsuccessfully and then called for an ambulance. I believe they called you in. That is really all I know.'

'So your impression was that this last row was all about Mrs Kennedy's drinking? Nothing to do with Mr Hislop?'

'No, Inspector. He did not mention Hislop on the phone last night.'

'Thank you Mr Waldren. You've been most helpful. I would like you to make a statement. If you would just put in your own words what you have told me, the sergeant will take you to a room where you can write it down without interruption. There may be one or two more questions after I have spoken to your wife so if you would be good enough to stay in the building. If you would like some tea or coffee Sergeant Parsons will organize it. Thank you for your co-operation, Mr Waldren.'

Sergeant Parsons took Tom to an empty interview room and left him with pens and a pile of statement paper. He dictated the preamble about the statement being made of Tom's free will and ordered him a cup of coffee.

Inspector Hoskings rang the front office and asked for a woman detective constable to bring Liz to his office. Liz had been sitting nervously for what had seemed like ages while Tom was being interviewed and was relieved by the appearance of the pretty woman detective constable. She introduced herself as Sue Brown and told Liz not to worry. The inspector was a sweetie she said and anyway she would be there throughout the interview to see fair play. When they walked into Inspector Hoskings' office he immediately asked if she would like a cup of tea or coffee. Liz accepted a coffee and they exchanged pleasantries until it arrived. The Inspector then explained that he was seeking background information to help him decide what charge or charges should be brought against Gilbert, that Liz was one of the last people to see Jane alive and that her recollection of their lunch together could be most helpful. After the formalities Inspector Hoskings asked, 'Would you have described Mrs Kennedy as a good friend?'

'Yes.'

'Was it a long-term friendship?'

'Not really. We had known each other for three years or so but it was on this last holiday that we got to know each other really well.'

'Why was this last holiday different from the previous ones?'

161

'I saw much more of her anyway but last weekend the rest of them went off to another golf course near Valencia and Jane and I decided to stay and saw a lot of each other.'

'Why did you and Mrs Kennedy not go with the others?'

Liz felt herself colouring and knew the inspector had noticed. 'Well, I don't like hotels much and Jane was very keen on her tennis, so we decided to stay.'

'And did you stay?'

Liz felt herself blushing again.

'Well, no. Actually we didn't. We went to Murcia because there is a lovely shop there – a sort of Spanish Harrods – and also one of the best restaurants in Spain.' Her words were tumbling out. 'I had always wanted to go there but Tom and Gilbert were always playing golf and so we thought it was a good opportunity to do both while our husbands were away. They knew all about it and were quite happy. Look, I've got the bill here from the hotel.' She rummaged in her handbag and triumphantly put the Rincon de Pepe bill on the desk. 'Look – Habitacion, that's room – Cena, that's dinner – Bar and Desayuno – that's breakfast.' Inspector Hoskings barely glanced at the bill and passed it back to her.

'And it was just the two of you who went to Murcia?'

'Yes, I've just said so, I've shown you the bill, for two.'

'Mr Hislop was not there as well?'

Liz paused, blushing again.

'You see Mrs Waldren, Mr Kennedy says that on their way home from here last night Mrs Kennedy taunted him by saying that it wasn't just you and her that went to Murcia last Saturday but Mr Hislop and Mr – he looked down at his notes – Mr Seddon as well and that it was nice that someone still found her attractive and did not moan about her drinking all the time. Mr Kennedy says that when they got home and she immediately poured herself a

162

large brandy, on top of all this, something snapped and for the first and only time in his life he struck Mrs Kennedy hard on the face. She fell back and caught her head on one of their fire dogs. Now, Mrs Waldren, did Mrs Kennedy make her story up or is Mr Kennedy lying or have you not told me the whole truth?'

'Oh, my God!' Liz put her hands over her face and could feel tears running between her fingers on to the carpet. Detective Brown came over with a box of tissues.

'Don't be upset, Mrs Waldren,' she said. 'You are not on trial. We just need to know all the background so that we can judge if Mr Kennedy has been telling us the truth.'

'Yes,' the Inspector added. 'The police may be interested in adultery as a background to a crime but not in the adultery itself. I can assure you that your part in the weekend should never become public knowledge but if a husband hits his wife because he has found out about her adultery, that is a blow with which any judge and jury would have sympathy and if you can confirm that Mrs Kennedy and Mr Hislop shared a room at this hotel and perhaps that Mrs Kennedy has told you that she and Mr Hislop made love, this could help Mr Kennedy.'

'But what about Tom?' Liz wailed. 'Will he have to know?'

'Not unless you choose to tell him, but he loves you very much Mrs Waldren and if you tell him, you may feel better but I think it will hurt him very deeply.'

Liz dabbed her eyes and blew her nose before looking up at the Inspector.

'Now, Mrs Waldren, shall we start again. I am not interested in what you did last weekend but to your certain knowledge did Mrs Kennedy and Mr Hislop share a room at the Hotel Rincon de Pepe last Saturday?'

'Yes.'

'And has Mrs Kennedy told you that they made love?'

163

'Yes.'

'Was Mrs Kennedy drinking heavily on the occasions you saw her during the last three weeks?'

'Yes.'

'Did Mrs Kennedy tell you that Mr Kennedy suspected her of having been unfaithful?'

'Yes.'

'Did Mr Kennedy have suspicions about the night in Murcia?'

'No, I don't think so, because I was there too and Jane concocted some story about a waiter having propositioned us which our husbands found totally credible. Also we spoke to our husbands from the hotel and in fact they rang us as well.'

'So when Mrs Kennedy told Mr Kennedy about a night of passion in Murcia, this would have been a double shock to him?'

'Yes, I suppose it would. My God. What a mess all this is.'

'I think that is all, Mrs Waldren. Thank you for being so frank. Detective Constable Brown will help you prepare a statement now, if you don't mind. There is no need to mention the hotel in Murcia, just that Mrs Kennedy had confided that she had committed adultery with Mr Hislop.'

'Thank you Inspector for being so understanding. I suppose this means that Gilbert knows that at best I was aiding and abetting Jane's adultery and that probably I was doing the same thing with . . .'

The Inspector interrupted. 'Yes, I am afraid it does but now he knows his own reaction to his wife's infidelity I think he is far too sensitive a man to tell your husband and risk him behaving in a similar way.'

'Thank God for that. I think you are probably right. What sort of charge will Gilbert face, Inspector? He is such a nice man.'

'It is not up to me to decide this but I would say the chances are that a charge of manslaughter will be preferred in view of the mitigating circumstances. He is certainly suffering very deeply now.'

'And what will happen to him now, before the trial?'

'I think his daughter has asked if he can stay with her and the police will not object to bail in all the circumstances.'

'Thank you again Inspector. You've been very kind.'

Sue Brown led her away and they met Tom in the passage.

'I suppose you've got to make a statement now, have you?' Tom noticed her red eyes. 'Are you OK love?'

'Yes, I'm all right. I just got a bit upset. Yes, I am just going to write my statement but it should not take long. Have you finished yours?'

'Yes,' Tom replied. He turned to Sue Brown. 'Do you know if the Inspector will want to see me again, officer?'

'No, I don't think so, sir. If you would like to wait downstairs or in your car. Your wife will not be very long.'

Sue helped Liz prepare a short statement which merely confirmed that Jane had been drinking heavily not only on the day in question but for some time beforehand and that she had told Liz of her adultery with James, without being specific as to when and where.

Liz found Tom waiting in the car listening to the radio which he turned off as she got into the car.

'Was that awful?' he said.

'Pretty awful, but I must say the Inspector was jolly nice and that detective constable was absolutely sweet. It could have been much worse. Apparently Gilbert should get bail to live with his daughter and they will probably bring a charge of manslaughter.'

'Oh, really. He didn't tell me that.'

'You probably didn't ask darling. I asked.'

165

'Touché. Well I don't suppose that is too bad in all the circumstances but it's bloody awful all the same. One thing all this has taught me is that we are not going to La Manga in that sort of set-up again. Next time it will be just us, unless Peter or Jean and her new husband want to come. I'll only play in the medals and stablefords and we'll do much more together. Go on trips. Go swimming perhaps from one of those deserted coves behind the Lion Mountain. You might even take advantage of me there, if they are as deserted as they say.' Tom smiled at her and squeezed her hand. 'And of course if you have a handicap by then there will be the Friday fourballs. I'd love a partner who gets lots of strokes.'

'We'll see, Tom – I know you – you'll meet some other blokes down there and some sort of challenge will be issued and you won't be able to resist. Still it may be the other way round now I've started. Maybe I'll be playing every day and you'll be the golf widower doing the shopping, cleaning the flat, preparing the meals. That wouldn't half shake you.'

'It certainly would. Shall we stop somewhere and have tea?'

'Oh, that would be lovely Tom. I can't think when you last took me out to tea.'

They found a small tea room and gorged themselves on fresh scones with strawberry jam and whipped cream.

'I dread to think what this is doing for my figure. It's just as well we do only go out to tea about every twenty-five years. I'm sure the last time was when we were courting.'

'I think your figure is just great.'

'That's what I'm worried about,' Liz laughed.

'Just perfect then. Just nicely rounded. I love you such a lot. I couldn't help thinking when I was writing that statement how empty my life would be if anything

166

happened to you . . . or if you left me,' he added almost as an afterthought.

'Well, I'm not leaving you Tom, so I think we're stuck with each other and I'm very happy about that.'

They spent a happy weekend with Jean and her fiancé coming to supper on Sunday and they discussed wedding plans in some detail. On Monday Tom went off to work as usual and at eight forty the telephone rang.

'Oxted 32157.'

'Hi, Liz. How are you?'

'Tony! I thought it might be you. The most awful thing has happened.'

Liz explained the whole story of Jane and Gilbert and her interview with the Inspector.

'God, how dreadful for you. Does this mean that our names are likely to be mentioned at the trial?'

'No, the Inspector didn't think so assuming Gilbert pleads guilty and I'm sure he will. He did say that adultery is not a crime in which the police are interested, Tony.'

'Thank God for that, talking of which, when can we see each other?'

'Tony, I don't think it is a good idea. It was wonderful and you made me feel a real woman and years younger than my age but I know if I saw you again we'd finish up in bed and if we did it once we'd do it again . . . and again and it would be lies and more lies and, Tony, although I long for your body more than I can say, I do love Tom and I want to stay with him. He has been ever so sweet this last week or so and last night my daughter and her fiancé came round and it was so . . . oh, so family and I loved it. Can you understand?'

'Yes, of course I can. Tom is a nice guy but don't think the longing is just one-sided and I would love to think that one day or night, without any risk or lies we might have an opportunity to fulfil each other again the way no one else ever has before.'

'Oh, so do I, but Tony, we must not look for that opportunity or we will make it happen and that would be wrong. It would have to be by pure chance.'

'OK, if you say so but I believe people make their own luck.'

'I'm not listening to you, Tony. Just talking to you makes my resolve weaker but it was great getting to know you so well and I thank you for my golf lessons. I'm really going to give it a go.'

'A refresher course at Sheringham would be entirely free . . . but with obligation.'

'I'm not listening. Goodbye Tony,' Liz said and put the phone down firmly. She was trembling and felt quite weak at the knees. She went through to the living room and sat down. She wondered how often Tony might phone. She hoped not too often as she was not sure she could always be so strong. If he rang when she was bored or when she and Tom were not getting on too well or if Tom were away on a golf trip what then? This time it had been quite easy because she and Tom were very close and he had been so supportive with the police interviews and everything.

She would really like to talk it over with someone but Jane would have been the obvious choice and she was dead. Who else was there? It must be someone with experience of an extra marital affair, someone worldly wise who had not always been the perfect wife and mother and who knew temptation and had perhaps succumbed to it. She racked her brains. Carol – Carol Grant. She was about her age and had been divorced a couple of years ago and she had married the chap with whom she had had the affair. She would be perfect. She looked in her diary and found her number. She dialled.

'Hello, this is Carol.'

'Carol, Liz Waldren here. How are you?'

'Oh, hi Liz. I'm fine thanks. Are you coming to NADFAS on Wednesday?'

'Yes, the talk is on antique drinking glasses isn't it? I'm looking forward to it. Look, Carol, are you doing anything this morning? Could you come and have a coffee?'

'Yes, why not? It'll make a nice break from housework. At your place or in town?'

'Oh, come here will you. You can have some Spanish coffee. About ten thirty? Is that OK?'

'Yes, fine. See you then. Bye.'

Liz felt better already. Carol was very sensible and was known as a straight talker. She would give her good advice. She washed up the breakfast things, went upstairs, showered, got dressed, made the bed and put the coffee on.

Carol was very unlike Liz to look at. Tall and slim with long legs, elegant clothes, highlighted hair and quite a lot of make up even at ten thirty in the morning. Liz had met her originally through NADFAS and they had become good friends over the years often shopping together or meeting in town for a coffee. They sat in the lounge and made inconsequential conversation for a few minutes while Liz poured the coffee. Carol lit a cigarette.

'Now Liz, what's on your mind? You didn't ask me over to discuss the price of vegetables at Tesco.'

'No, you're right. I didn't. I wanted to ask your advice. This is in strict confidence you understand.'

'Yes, of course. Go on.'

'Well, when we were in Spain I met this chap and . . .' It all came tumbling out and Carol listened patiently with just the odd interjection to clarify a point.

'So, what do you think?' Liz finished breathlessly.

'It sounds awfully like the story of Derek and me really, except we had our affair locally and not in Spain and we were found out and now it is Derek and me and not David and me, but believe me it's never worth it, not for people who are about fifty anyway. In their thirties or early forties perhaps because people change so much in their twenties and thirties, but at our age – no way José. At the time of the affair it is, or you think it is, the excitement – the danger – not being able to keep your hands off each other. At our age having it off three or four times a night, and every time a different way. It's inventive, it's explorative, it's oral. You know what they say about oral sex, do you? It's a bit like lobster thermidor – you don't often have either at home.'

They both laughed.

'But honestly, Liz, it doesn't last. Don't get me wrong. I'm not knocking Derek. He is a good chap, but so was David. We got on all right. Not that different from you and Tom I shouldn't think, but really the only differences now are all bad. We're less well off. I've lost a few friends inevitably because they took David's side and think it would be disloyal to see me as well. David and I don't see the children as often because for them either it means an all day trip so they can have lunch with one and dinner with the other or two trips close together so one of us does not feel missed out and for David or me to visit them is that much more of an effort going on one's own and we used to often combine a visit with something else. I preferred my old house and I miss a lot of the antiques David and I bought together. I know that sounds petty but I can't help it. I suppose at the moment Derek and I do make more effort to please each other than David and I did, but will we after eighteen or twenty years? I doubt it.

'I'm not saying no one in their fifties should get divorced. Of course they should. They may just be wrong for each other in some way but David and I weren't and you and Tom aren't. David didn't beat me up. He wasn't unfaithful, or if he was he was very discreet and it certainly wasn't on a regular basis. We were good parents and had a good relationship with the children. It's just that when the children left home I had more time on my hands and I was bored, and from what you say you were bored and felt neglected. It wasn't much of a holiday for you. It was a holiday for Tom when he did everything he wanted and you had time on your hands. But boredom alone is not a good reason for divorce and it is largely self-inflicted. If you feel bored you must ask yourself why you are bored and what you can do about it. Nearly always you can do something and it does not have to be something as dramatic as taking a lover.'

'So what do I do now, Carol?'

'Well, I think you thank God for a fantastic week in your life which hasn't done you or Tom any harm. Probably a bit of good really because he is not going to take you for granted so much again and then you must – yes, you must write to Tony – I don't think you should see him or telephone him because I don't think your resolve is strong enough yet – and tell him shortly but definitely and clearly that it is all over and you do not want him to contact you again. If he is a decent bloke, and from what you say it sounds as if he is, he will accept that and you can get on with your life with Tom. You see, for you it would be even worse than for me if you split up, because you would presumably have to go to Norfolk miles away from your friends and interests here. I don't think you would find that easy at your age. Starting a new life in your twenties is fine but at fifty odd? And do you know that Tony would want you on a permanent basis? You didn't say he had ever suggested that. Just that he wanted to see you again. He may be quite happy as he is.'

'Hm, thank you Carol. I think you have confirmed what I was thinking myself but I wanted reassurance and

171

I thought you would be just the right person to ask. Another coffee?'

'Yes, thanks. I'm quite thirsty after all that talking.'

They had another coffee and soon afterwards Carol left.

No time like the present, Liz thought, and went over to her writing desk. She got out a sheet of notepaper and began to write.

> My dear Tony,
> I want to thank you for a wonderful week, a week when I felt young again and experienced feelings and emotions which had lain dormant for years, but, Tony, I have thought very hard this last week and I want you to believe me when I say it was a holiday romance and it is over. I don't want it to continue in England so if you feel anything for me please do not try and contact me again.
>
> Tom and I love each other and the life we lead together and I do not want anything to spoil that. So goodbye Tony and thank you for everything, including the awakening of an interest in playing golf. I shall carry on with that and will always have that to remember you by.
>
> Liz.

She read the letter through, addressed the envelope, sealed and stamped it and took it to the pillar box at the end of the road before she could change her mind.

What could she do for Tom? she wondered. She wanted to show him how much she loved him. What would he like for supper? Avocado with prawns for a starter and then wing of skate with black butter sauce and a few French beans and a bottle of Chablis. He would like that she thought and he did.

He helped her clear away the supper things and wash up while the coffee percolated.

'That really was a wonderful meal. All my favourites. You do spoil me.'

'It's just I realise how lucky I am to have you and our life together and you were so sweet to me on Saturday. It was no more than you deserve. I keep thinking of poor Gilbert and Jane.'

'Yes, I've thought a lot about them too. We must keep in touch with Gilbert, have him over for a meal and show we don't blame him for the tragedy and of course we must go to the funeral. We could ask him then.'

They did keep in regular touch with Gilbert and once when he and Liz were alone he said, 'You know I would never say anything to Tom about Murcia.'

Liz put her hand on his. 'Thank you, Gilbert. I never thought you would and it is all over. I won't see Tony again.'

Gilbert's case came up at Guildford Crown Court about four months later when he pleaded guilty to the charge of manslaughter as the Inspector had predicted.

The prosecution very fairly but briefly and without detail presented the extenuating circumstances leading up to the fatal blow and also that the autopsy had revealed that the blow could not have been very hard as there was no evidence of heavy bruising or contusions and that in the normal way such a blow would not have caused any serious injury.

The defence produced medical evidence to show that Jane's heavy drinking could have impaired her sense of balance to some extent. The sentence of the court was that Gilbert should carry out two hundred and forty hours community service.